## Annabelle wasn't about to bare her soul to Ben...

...regardless of the wine, or the moonlight, or the effect of the inescapable charm of the man seated next to her.

But unexpectedly her chest ached, and she felt as if she might be going to cry. She fought against it, panicking at her loss of control. Why should his gentle touch evoke such a depth of feeling in her? How could he unerringly pinpoint all the things that she knew were missing in her life?

She took another sip of her wine. God. The wine was making her careless. She allowed herself to fantasize about being in his arms. Her breath quickened and her body grew warm.

Ben reached over and covered her hand with his own. He looked questioningly into her eyes, but remained silent.

It was too painful to meet his gaze. Annabelle looked away. So many of her dreams had shrivelled and died over the years. A fierce longing suddenly seized her. Why had she never pursued happiness the way Ben seemed to have done?

# 1

"EXCUSE ME, CAN YOU help me? I seem to be lost."

The moment Annabelle Murdoch rolled down the car window, a blast of sweltering July heat overpowered her car's air-conditioning system. Her antiperspirant succumbed without a struggle, and she felt droplets of sweat begin to form on her forehead and between her breasts.

She swore under her breath. She was nervous about this meeting, and she wanted to at least look cool and calm.

The young boy she'd stopped leaned low on his handlebars and stared in at her. He was panting, and his freckled face was red and sweaty, just the way hers was going to be any second now. A mop of carrot-colored hair lay glued to his forehead. He wore cut-off jean shorts and what had once been a white undershirt.

"Can you tell me where the Baxter place is? I thought it was here on Middlebench Road, but I can't seem to locate it." No damn wonder. Some of the residents of Oyama didn't seem to find it necessary to mark their properties with either numbers or names—a practice that infuriated Annabelle. It would make a real-estate person's life so much easier if people would only be methodical about things. Annabelle knew the value of order; after all, she'd built a successful real-estate business by paying meticulous attention to detail.

"Ben's place?" The boy grinned at her, displaying front teeth far too big for his mouth. "Hey, I live right next door to Ben. Sure, lady, just follow me. I'll show ya. I was goin' up there anyhow."

Before Annabelle could say another word, he was pumping along the gravel road ahead of her, his narrow back bent and bony elbows sticking out as he sped along. His energy made her feel even more enervated.

She rolled her window back up and irritably jacked the air-conditioning to High, then found a tissue and patted away the sweat beads that had popped out on her face. She lifted one arm and then the other to check for perspiration stains, exhaling a relieved breath when none were apparent.

The boy was peddling like a maniac up a slight incline now, and she hoped he didn't feel he had to speed along this way for her sake. He'd get heatstroke for sure if he kept this up, especially with his coloring.

She had auburn hair and fair skin herself—a legacy from her Celtic ancestors—and she figured she was the Okanagan's best customer when it came to sun block and lotion. She'd grown up in England, where the weather was cool and moderate, and at times like this she really missed that temperate climate. It was impossible to stay calm and collected when the temperature hovered in the high nineties like this, day after day. Other years she hadn't minded it so much, but this year the unremitting heat seemed the last straw in a series of circumstances over which she had no control.

With a beckoning wave, her guide turned off the gravel road onto a dirt track, then veered into a barely visible opening in a tall hedge. Muttering under her breath about reclusive old coots and impossible places to find, Annabelle steered carefully after him, wincing each time her low-slung car bottomed out on the rutted road.

The boy stopped halfway down the lane to open a rickety gate. He carefully stood aside so she could drive through, and locked it again after them. She smiled at him and waved a thank-you.

Now they were in an orchard. Apple trees, their copious fruit still green, dotted a hillside. The trail—and that was a dignified description for what her poor little car was having to endure—wound its way in a peculiar pattern among the trees, until at last, after scaling a preposterously steep incline, the boy braked and jumped off his bike almost on the doorstep of a battered blue-and-white house trailer nestled among the fruit trees.

Annabelle automatically assessed it. The trailer's resale value would be next to zero, but the land it stood on was something else. It commanded a spectacular view; the entire valley lay far below, its panorama of lakes sparkling in the midmorning sunshine.

She pulled to a stop and sat for a moment, trying to still the nervous fluttering in her stomach. This meeting with Benjamin Baxter was crucial to her company, and she was determined to make it go well. She flipped down her visor and checked herself out in the mirror. As she'd known it would be, her face was flushed and her freckles were showing, but at least her short, sassy haircut was holding up. Her aqua silk slacks and matching top were no more creased than she'd expect them to be after an hour in the car. She could only hope her expensive cologne was still making a statement.

*Go get him, Annabelle Murdoch. You've handled tougher deals than this one, before.*

Tougher, maybe. But none of them had been quite as important as this. God, she needed Ben Baxter to be agreeable.

She took a deep breath, grabbed her eelskin briefcase, and slid gracefully out, suddenly aware that the boy was banging quite rudely on the closed trailer door. Anxiety and irritation filled her. She wanted above all to make a good impression on Mr. Baxter.

"Excuse me, please don't do that—" The sentence ended in a garbled scream. A huge German shepherd came hurtling toward her around the corner of the trailer, barking ferociously. But it wasn't just the dog that terrified her.

Behind the dog trotted two huge animals with long necks, small heads, banana-shaped ears and protruding eyes. They looked like a mismatch between an ostrich and a camel, and without a pause, they headed straight for her.

She wasn't good with animals. In fact, she was downright afraid of them. She made a mad leap into her car, scrambling in and slamming the door just as the trio closed in on her. She'd dropped her briefcase outside, and the three creatures trod blithely over it. The dog halted beside her door and put two huge paws on the side of the car, staring in at her and whining. The other two beasts walked around the car, bending elongated necks, tilting huge ears forward and peering in at her with expressions of mild curiosity on their faces. They had the longest eyelashes she had ever seen.

She was trembling, and she realized she was going to have to use a bathroom fairly soon.

The boy came rushing over, scolding at the top of his lungs. He grabbed the dog by its collar and dragged it away. The other two animals followed him, quite docilely, and as her breathing slowly steadied, Annabelle recognized that they were llamas.

The boy was back now, leaning down and hollering at her through the closed windows. With the motor off, the car was an airless oven, and icy sweat ran down between her breasts. It was either smother in here or venture out again.

She opened the door an inch, looking around cautiously this time.

"It's okay now, miss, honest. Those llamas broke outta the pen again, but I got them corralled. They'll be okay fer a while. I tied Susie up. Y'know, the dog? She jumps up on you, but it's just because she's real friendly. She only looks vicious. Ben's tryin' ta break her of jumpin', but it's slow goin'. I think she maybe scratched your car. Ben's prob'ly still sleeping. His motorcycle's out back so I know he's home."

Who in God's name could sleep through all this? Was Benjamin Baxter an invalid? What kind of person allowed his animals to attack visitors in this way? And now her beautiful car was scratched, too. She fought down a sense of outrage and anger, wanting nothing more than to start the engine and drive off. Instead she climbed out and headed for the trailer, struggling to hide her emotions under a professional veneer of good nature.

She was on the wooden steps leading to the door when it swung open, crashing all the way back against the side of the trailer. Another two steps and she would have been knocked senseless. She quickly stepped back down.

"Jason, what in bloody hell's going on out here? I've never heard such a racket—"

The bellow ended abruptly as his gaze met hers. He made an effort at clearing his throat, and then groaned, shutting his eyes and opening them again as if hoping she'd disappear in the interim.

"I don't believe this. Who in blazes are you?"

He was younger than she'd expected—not all that much older than her. He was half naked, mustached, and immense. Clearly he wasn't pleased about being awakened. His electric-blue eyes were swollen and bloodshot under thick dark brows that lifted at the outer corners, giving him the appearance of a bad-tempered satyr. It was obvious by the heavy stubble on his square jaw that he hadn't shaved, perhaps for days.

He was tanned a deep mahogany shade—all over.

Annabelle had to swallow hard at how much "all over" there was of him.

His bare chest was matted with curls that arrowed down to a pair of badly worn, blue-jean cutoffs cling-ing to narrow hips. The zipper was zipped, but the top snap was undone and gaping, and the garment rode dangerously low. Annabelle was several steps down, and she couldn't help but notice that he wore nothing under them. Everything . . . a great deal of every-thing . . . was clearly outlined under the worn denim.

Bare, tanned legs like well-shaped tree trunks led down to large and equally bare feet.

Instead of some old eccentric, as she'd expected, she was going to have to deal with this—this—

Words failed her. She'd never felt as out of place or uncomfortable in her entire life. She cleared her throat and tried to say something, but she was at a loss for words.

Jason turned from an intense inspection of her car and grinned.

"Hung on a good one last night, huh, Ben? I heard you guys over here laughin' fit to kill before I went to sleep. Man, you look somethin' awful this mornin'. Hey, Cupid and Clara got out again. He's figured out how to open that latch you put on the gate. I tied it shut with a piece of twine from the shed but I bet it don't hold him long. He's an escape artist, that Cupid. Man, this's some neat car, miss. Really low suspension. I heard you hittin' bottom on the way up. And, oh yeah, Ben, I tied up Susie. She jumped up on this lady's car. There's scratches all down the driver's side. gonna have to have some body work done. We gonna go swimmin' this afternoon like you said, Ben? It's hot as Hades. I'll go and feed the chickens and put water in the trough for the llamas while you make up your mind, okay?"

BEN CLUNG TO THE doorframe and tried to make sense out of the situation.

But it was damn difficult to concentrate when the pain behind his eyeballs felt like it would—any minute—pierce his brain and kill him. He massaged his throbbing temples and blinked hard. Here, standing before him on his doorstep, was the best looking woman he'd seen in a month of Sundays. He'd been fantasizing this very miracle for a while now, ever since his forty-fourth birthday, and the unexpected departure of Sasha, in fact. Turning forty-four had made him start wishing he'd meet a different kind of woman than Sasha. She'd been great in the sack, but out of it, her conversational abilities were limited.

So why did a woman like this one have to appear now? God had a weird sense of humor, was all he could figure.

He needed water, and he needed a lot of it right away. Along with extra-strength whatever-he-could-find-in-the-drawer-where-he-tossed-the-aspirin. If he could find the bloody drawer. The sun was frying whatever part of his brain Rico's home brew hadn't already destroyed. And to top it off, his stomach suddenly rebelled.

"Come in, please. Shut that door behind you or the animals'll be inside and the air-conditioning will quit. I'll be right back."

He turned on his heel and made a beeline for the bathroom at the back of the trailer. He had just enough time to turn the radio beside his bed to full volume on his way past—thank Providence it was permanently set to a rock station that played golden oldies. Loud.

He slammed the bathroom door behind him and retched painfully to Fats Domino singing "Ain't That a Shame." Then he turned the shower to cold, and stuck his head and torso under the icy spray.

Three glasses of water, an attack on his mouth with the toothbrush, and two extra-strength something-or-others gave him faint hope that just maybe he could now face the woman waiting in the front of the trailer. He pulled on an almost-white T-shirt that was conveniently hanging on the towel rack, snapped the top button of his cutoffs and went to greet his guest. Fats had given way to the noon news, so he turned the radio off.

She was sitting on his couch, one elegant silky leg crossed over the other, hands folded in graceful precision in her lap, doing her best to ignore the empty wine bottles and sticky glasses and scattered playing cards and half-empty potato-chip bags strewn around his living area.

She got hastily to her feet when he appeared. She gave him a wide, phony smile that didn't get anywhere near her eyes—eyes that were chocolate brown and wary—and held out her hand. He took it in his and held on as long as she allowed. Her hand was narrow, and her skin felt soft against his calluses.

"Sorry about the mess," he tried to explain. "Had a little get-together here last night. With some friends. It lasted pretty late." He was nowhere near lucid, so he gave up and just looked at her, instead.

She was great to look at. The green outfit she wore sort of slipped and slithered over voluptuous curves, and she had hair that looked exactly like a rusty, up-side-down chrysanthemum. He wished fervently that he was in better shape to appreciate her.

"Sit down, please," he urged when she withdrew her hand. She came to just below his chin, probably five-seven or thereabouts—a perfect female size when you were six foot and a couple of inches.

She cleared her throat. "My name is Murdoch, Mr. Baxter. Annabelle Murdoch. I'm sorry to disturb you, but I did try to call before I came. Numerous times, in fact, but there was never any answer. Perhaps your phone is out of order?"

She glanced over at the old-fashioned black telephone on the kitchen counter. The cord wasn't connected to the wall.

"I leave it unplugged most of the time, except for when I need to use it," he said. "I figure phones either control you, or you control them, right?"

She frowned, and appeared shocked. "But what if there's an important call?"

"I don't get important calls."

She had a beguiling accent, an English accent. English accents always intrigued him. They were sexy as hell.

Her deep brown eyes flicked down him and up again, and he realized that his shorts were soaking wet from the dousing in the shower. "Look…umm, Anna. Belle. Sit down. I'll make some coffee."

It wasn't easy. He dumped the old grounds from the machine and made a fresh pot, hands trembling, having to concentrate on the usually routine steps. He washed out two mugs from the collection in the sink and dried them carefully. He felt the need to explain to her that it wasn't always this way around here.

"My friend Rico makes his own home brew. I had some last night and I swear to God it causes brain damage. If I had any sense, I'd stick to my own homemade wine. No one ever gets a hangover from my wine. I make it the old-fashioned way—no chemicals or additives, just grapes and good water, the way my grandfather did. Maybe you'd like a glass instead of coffee? It's pretty hot out for coffee."

She shook her head. "Coffee's fine, thank you." She hesitated, and then blurted, "Could I possibly use your bathroom?" She looked mortified at having to ask.

"Sure." He gestured down the hall. "On your right." He tried to remember how bad the mess in the bathroom was, and decided there wasn't a damn thing he could do about it anyway.

What the hell. She'd probably seen men's underwear before.

She wasn't gone long. She sat down again and was blessedly quiet while he fumbled around in the kitchen. When at last the machine began making its comforting, gurgling noises, he dared to ease himself into an armchair facing her.

She was watching him with an uneasy expression on her face. It seemed imperative that she understand that he wasn't always this way—hung over, living in the midst of chaos. He did his best once again to explain what had happened.

"Had a couple of friends over last night. One of them's a writer and he just sold his first book. Not the first one Amos's written, just the first one he's sold. A mystery. Well, I haven't read it yet, but Amos says it's a mystery."

God, he was incapable of ordinary speech today. He made a monumental effort and tried again. "Anyhow, it was a memorable occasion. Amos's been writing for years and never got a bite till now, and I guess I drank a bit too much. We all did." He attempted a deprecatory laugh, but it came out sounding more like a bray.

"Mr. Baxter..."

"Ben. Call me Ben."

"Ben." She drew in a deep breath, and even in his frazzled state, he noticed it did wonderful things for the silk covering her breasts.

Why the hell did a hangover make him horny? It should have exactly the opposite effect.

She smiled, big and wide and friendly. "Ben, I'm with Midas Realty, in Kelowna."

A real-estate agent. Disappointment was a natural reaction, he supposed. She wasn't the first who'd come scouting around; almost anyone with twenty acres of view property in the Okanagan had been approached lately with offers. She was just the first real-estate agent he'd met with any sex appeal.

Annabelle saw his expression change, become guarded and remote. For a fleeting instant, she felt regret. He'd been looking at her the way a man looks at a woman he admires, and even though it was unsettling, it was also flattering.

Not that she was interested; he was definitely not her type.

Or at least he wouldn't be, if she'd ever had a type. And the way he lived appalled her; skimpy black and red underwear tossed in every corner of the bathroom, shirts hanging on doorknobs, wet towels piled in the tub—to say nothing of the chaos out here. But he was attractive. There was no denying that.

*Remember what you're here for, and how important it is. Charm, Annabelle, charm.*

She cleared her throat. "My partners and I are interested in a piece of property you own on the west side of Okanagan Lake. I believe it's called Likely Cove?"

He raised an eyebrow. "I'm surprised. I thought it would be this property you wanted." The coffee was ready. He got up, filled two mugs and handed her one. "Cream? Sugar?"

She shook her head. "Black's fine, thank you."

He hadn't really responded at all to her statement, so she tried again. "We're prepared to make you a generous offer for the cove, even though the land surrounding it is privately owned. The cove itself is quite worthless as far as development goes. I'm sure you're aware of that—it's much too rocky even for a beach house. But the party who owns the acreage is interested in acquiring the cove, strictly for access purposes." She wasn't about to reveal that it was another of her companies, Pinetree Developments, that owned the acreage. "Would you consider selling, Ben?"

Her stomach tightened and her heart began to hammer so hard she wondered if it showed through her blouse. She struggled to keep her features from revealing anything but the most nonchalant degree of interest.

Her years in real estate had made her adept at hiding her true feelings, thank God, but it took every ounce of experience and self-control to look relaxed about this.

Because he *had* to sell her the cove, or her business would be bankrupt in a matter of months. She'd lose everything she'd worked so hard to attain; and most devastating of all, Theodore would know she'd failed after all.

Theodore Winslow was her ex-husband and her major competitor in the local real-estate market. She considered him her arch enemy. The idea of failing, and having Theodore as a gleeful witness to her failure, made the coffee she swallowed taste like bile in her throat.

"Sorry. I'm not about to sell any of my property, particularly the cove." His response was immediate, and her heart plummeted.

He went on after a moment: "I have a soft spot for that place, you see."

She forced a smile and tried for an offhand tone. "Oh? Why is that, Ben?"

There had to be a way to make him change his mind, and the best thing to do was to get to know him a little, find out what his reasons were for refusing to sell, find out what motivated him, discover the chink in his armor that would allow her to get what she wanted—what she *needed*, in order to survive.

He rested his coffee cup on the arm of his chair. "Well, the cove makes it simple for me to get out to Paradise."

"Paradise?" She shook her head, confused.

"That's my name for the island. That little island out in the middle of Okanagan Lake, the one sort of adjacent to Likely Cove?"

"Oh. Oh, yes. I remember now. But it's called Otter Island, on my maps."

He nodded, sipping the last of his coffee. "Technically, yeah, that's the legal name for it, although I couldn't say why. Never laid eyes on an otter over there. The name didn't do the place justice, so I renamed it Paradise."

"So you own the island, as well as the cove?" She was doing her level best to keep the conversation easy and flowing, without letting him know she was digging for all the information she could get. Knowledge was power.

He nodded, and it must have hurt his head because he screwed his eyes shut for a moment and sucked in a breath before he answered. "Yeah, I do. I won them both in a poker game, let's see, must be at least ten years ago now."

She laughed, hoping it didn't sound as contrived to him as it did to her. "That's an unusual way to acquire real estate, isn't it? How'd it happen, Ben?" She leaned forward, resting her arms on her knees, deliberately using body language to create an aura of intimacy, trying to inject a lively sparkle into her eyes.

It must have worked because he smiled at her, and she noticed how it changed his features, softening the wide, thin-lipped mouth under the mustache, bringing the hint of a twinkle to those arresting blue eyes.

"Guess it is sort of offbeat, all right. Actually, I was still in the force at the time—the RCMP—stationed in Bella Coola. This other corporal and I got in a game with the fellow who owned the local hotel—Maddigan was his name—and he hit a losing streak. I actually won his boat, but I traded him for the cove and the island, instead. Hell, he really loved that boat."

"How long were you a policeman?" The information had surprised her. The last thing she'd have suspected was that he'd been an RCMP officer. He certainly didn't look like one right now. Although he did have an air about him, of self-confidence and strength.

"Twenty years. I retired and moved here four years ago."

"And are you considering a second career?" He seemed far too young for full retirement, and it would help if she knew something about his financial circumstances. She could always sweeten the offer. "Lots of retired policemen seem to get into real estate, for instance. I know several in Kelowna."

His smile widened, and there was a magnetism about it that made her want to smile back. "Not me. I'm committed to being a born-again hippie, Anna. Belle. Annabelle. Is that all one name, or is it two?"

"It's two, actually, but I use it as one. I was named for both of my grandmothers."

"I like it. It has a nice old-fashioned ring to it."

As soon as he'd said it, Ben watched soft color suffuse her face. So she wasn't comfortable with compliments, even those as innocent as the one he'd just paid her. You'd think she'd be used to flattery, attractive as she was, Ben reflected.

And she *was* attractive. Redheads like her usually had pinkish complexions, but hers was sort of a light honey color instead, smooth and glowing, with an intriguing amount of freckles across her straight nose. Dramatic dark brown eyebrows, like her eyes. Big eyes, with golden lights in the irises. Nice dark eyelashes too, long and curly. And where was the brassy polish a high-powered career woman ought to have?

He got up to refill his cup, gesturing with the pot at hers, as well. She shook her head no, and he filled his own, grateful for the numbing effect the caffeine and painkillers were having on his hangover.

"You lived in Kelowna long, Annabelle?"

He could tell right away she wasn't comfortable with him asking her questions. She sat back and crossed her legs, fiddling with the bracelet on her right wrist. She met his eyes all right, but there was a guarded expression there.

Well, what the hell. She'd asked more than a few. He figured it was his turn.

"I've lived here for eleven years."

"You came here as an infant?" He thought she might smile at that bit of outright blarney, but he was mistaken. Again, she met his gaze directly enough, but there was no hint of a smile. She was guarded. All the same, there was something vulnerable about her, though, under that businesslike exterior.

"Actually, I was twenty-four years old when I came here."

He could still add. That made her thirty-five. He was delighted. Thirty-five was a perfect age for women, in his opinion.

"Still just a kid." He kept on trying to tease her a little, break down that barrier of seriousness she'd erected the moment he took control of the conversation.

She shook her head. "Hardly."

"Married?" Damn, he shouldn't have asked that. It made him sound like some middle-aged jerk who was on the make. He cursed his clumsiness.

She gave him a long, cool look and then said, simply and finally, "No."

"Me either." He tried to cover his blunder. "I tried it once, but it didn't work out too well."

She met his eyes with that steady, sober gaze, but didn't volunteer anything. It was like pulling teeth, getting anything out of her, but he persevered. "So you came here to the Okanagan straight from England?"

This time there was the faintest trace of an enigmatic smile.

"Not straight by any means, but originally, yes. Now, how did you guess that I was English?"

He found that his lips were starting to work again. They'd actually stretched into a grin without affecting his eyes. "My incredible investigative abilities. Of course, your accent had nothing to do with it."

She nodded, and the tension between them began to ease a little. "It always amazes me that people think I have an accent, you know? I've always thought everyone here in B.C. except me had very decided accents."

This was getting better and better. He raised an eyebrow at her. "Like the doting mother watching the parade? My Johnny's the only one in step."

Now he was rewarded with a wide, crooked smile that had something strangely melancholy about it. She had lovely even teeth, very white. The smile made her eyes look sad, because it didn't reach that far.

"Something like that, yes."

For a comfortable moment, they were quiet. Ben could hear Jason outside, whistling cheerfully to the chickens.

Then she seemed to get tense all over again, uncrossing her legs and leaning forward, all business. "Perhaps if I present my offer, you might reconsider about the cove, Ben. It's quite generous." She named a figure that sounded high, even at today's inflated prices. He said nothing.

"It's good until the end of July, three weeks from now. You will give it some thought?"

He hated ending it all this way, but honesty demanded that he be straight and up front about it. "There's no way I'll ever sell the cove, Annabelle, no way at all. It's my access route to the island, you see. I keep an old boat in a ramshackle boathouse there in Likely Cove, and I can just drive over, hop in the boat and be on Paradise in an hour."

"I'm quite sure a mutually agreeable solution for your boat could be negotiated—"

"But I'm just not interested." He cut off whatever she'd been about to say, sorry that the earlier rapport was gone, but he was determined to forestall any more real-estate talk.

"I don't need the money I'd get for selling the cove, and there's simply no incentive whatsoever for me to do so. I'm a creature of habit. I like things exactly the way they are in regard to Likely Cove. I'd be wasting your time if I let you think otherwise."

He managed what he hoped was a provocative grin. "Not that it wouldn't be tempting to string you along a little, have you drive out here again to see me. You're a very attractive woman, Annabelle."

She didn't blush this time at all, and he was disappointed.

She smiled at him again, as she reached out and placed the papers with the offer on his coffee table. Then she gathered up her briefcase—battered looking and rather dirty—and got to her feet.

"I can only hope you'll reconsider, Ben. My card is there if you want to get in touch with me." She gestured at the papers and moved toward the trailer door.

Damn it all. She was getting away on him, and he couldn't think of any way to prevent it.

# 2

HE MOVED TO OPEN THE door for her, but she hesitated a moment before going outside.

"Those animals of yours, those . . . llamas. They, umm, they aren't . . . dangerous, are they?"

He laughed aloud, enjoying the contrast between the confident real-estate agent and the vulnerable woman. "Not at all. In fact, they're about the friendliest animals I've ever come across. They *are* pretty curious, though. And mischievous as all get-out." He remembered all of a sudden what Jason had been blabbing about a while before.

"Oh, hell. They probably tried to mob you when you first drove up, didn't they? Jason said they'd gotten loose again. They do that when people drive into the yard." Something else struck him. "Didn't he also say my German shepherd jumped on your car and scratched it?"

Maybe there was hope yet for a meeting that had nothing to do with real estate. She must be pretty steamed about the damage to her vehicle, even though she didn't show it. He hadn't paid a lot of attention, but it seemed to him she'd been driving a late-model sporty job.

"Your dog *did* jump up on the car," she confirmed in a neutral tone. He couldn't detect any irritation, but he'd bet it was there just under the surface. He'd bet she kept one hell of a lot under the surface, this Annabelle

Murdoch. There was this sense he got that she was reining in her real feelings all the time.

He followed her out, managing not to groan out loud when the sun struck him full force. "Jesus, it has to be over a hundred out here today—or whatever boiling is in metric. I never did get it straight."

"It's hot, all right, isn't it?" She stopped and gazed out at the breathtaking panorama of purple valleys and turquoise lakes that his property overlooked. "You have a million-dollar view from up here, Ben. If you ever wanted to develop this parcel, you'd end up a million-aire."

He looked out at it with her, annoyed and disappointed that she interpreted beauty only in terms of dollars and cents and parcels of subdividable land.

But after a moment the entire scene seemed to shimmer and shift in a white-hot haze. He'd almost forgotten about his hangover, but it was all coming back to him now. He'd also forgotten he was barefoot. He swore under his breath and limped across the gravel drive to have a look at the damage his half-witted dog had done.

Sure enough, there were dozens of faint toenail scratches in the glittering candy-red paint on the driver's side. It was a disgrace, having that happen to a car like this one—it was less than a year old. It was gleaming from a recent wash and polish, and the interior looked spanking clean, as well.

Well, it sure as hell gave him a reason to call her again, anyhow. He wouldn't blame her for being real put-out over the incident.

"I'm sorry, Annabelle. I'm gonna strangle that maniac animal with my bare hands one of these days. If you'll get an estimate on repairs on this, I'll pay. I'll be in touch with you about it in a day or so. My apologies."

She'd opened the car door and swung inside with one fluid motion. She looked up at him, about to close the door. "I'll find out. Perhaps my insurance will cover it and that'll be that. It's not important. But if you should have a change of heart about the cove, please do call me, won't you? Thank you for the coffee. Goodbye, now."

So the scratches weren't important, but the cove was? She had screwed-up values, for sure. He watched her back the car around and turn, and then negotiate his winding driveway at a snail's pace.

"Some car, huh, Ben? It's a Le Sabre, right? She drives it real careful. Man, if I had a car like that, I'd open 'er up, see what she could do." Jason was standing behind him, watching the sporty red car negotiate the turn onto Middlebench Road.

"That passion for speed is likely why you're restricted to a bike, Jase." Ben was frowning, trying to get a fix on Annabelle Murdoch. On the surface, she was cool, no doubt about that; she must have been mad as hell about Susie damaging her car, yet she hadn't revealed it. She'd done a good job of getting him to talk about himself, yet when he turned the tables on her, she pretty much clammed up. And there was that undercurrent of tension all the time, the sense he got of her being wound up tight as a spring, even though she was doing her damnedest to appear relaxed and easygoing about things. Years in the police force made him sensitive to people's real reactions. And maybe he was just open to a challenge.

She'd be a challenge, all right. No question there.

"Well, I only got two years and three months left till I can get my license," Jason was saying. He screwed his face up. "If Mom lets me, which I doubt. By then, the Volkswagen coupe will probably pack it in, and I'll never get a chance to drive."

Ben's thoughts were still on the woman who was winding her way along the country roads, the red car flashing into view now and then in between orchards and houses. "Think positive, kid. It's almost unheard of for a man to get through life without a driver's licence. I think you'll manage fine."

They watched in companionable silence as Annabelle made the hairpin turns down and around and down again to the valley bottom and the highway. When at last she'd disappeared completely among the thick green of the orchards, Ben heaved a sigh and turned back to the trailer.

"There's pop in the fridge. You want one, kid?"

"Yeah, please, I'm parched. I did the chickens and put out fresh water and stuff for Cupid and Clara. Oh yeah, the eggs. I left 'em in the pail at the side of the chicken house. I'll get 'em right now, and I'll untie Susie on the way past. She's havin' a fit back there. Then we gonna go swimmin' like you said, Ben?"

"You finish all your chores at home?"

"Heck, ya. Hours ago, while you were still sleepin'. I even left a note for Mom, so when she gets home from work she knows where I am."

"Then I guess we'll go swimming." The thought of cool green lake water was the first thing today that held any appeal at all.

Inside the trailer, the faint sweet scent of Annabelle Murdoch's perfume lingered.

The second thing. The lake was the second thing that had appealed to him today. The lady named Annabelle had definitely been alluring.

"Who was that woman, anyways, Ben?" Jason slammed the trailer door behind him, put the eggs in the fridge and extracted a cola, expertly popping the top open and guzzling half of it down without a pause.

"She's a real-estate person." He half wished it weren't so. Real estate demanded a certain kind of personality, and he didn't want to think she was typical.

Hell, she wasn't typical at all. There was nothing brash or grating about her, that was for sure. In fact, she'd seemed more than a little shy at times.

The boy set the cola down with a thump and turned frightened eyes on Ben. "You . . . you're not gonna sell out or anything, are you, Ben? You're not gonna move away, are ya?"

Ben reached out and ruffled Jason's thick red mop of hair.

Annabelle's hair was several shades darker, but just as vibrant. Just as thick, too, from the look of it. Softer, he'd guess, and maybe not quite so sweaty.

"Not on your life, kid. I spent half my life moving around. I plan to spend the second half right here."

Jason let out a huge sigh of relief and picked up his pop again. "I'm real glad. You really got it made, Ben, y'know? When I grow up, I'm gonna be a bachelor just like you—nobody to boss a guy around all the time and keep naggin' about stuff like clean underwear."

"Well, there're worse things than clean underwear, Jase."

Like having no one to notice whether it was clean or not. He spent a long, lecherous moment wondering about Annabelle's underwear. Would it be plain and utilitarian, or was he right about the sensuality she tried so hard to conceal? Maybe she'd wear flimsy scraps of satin and lace.... He was sweating, and the visions of female underwear had nothing to do with it.

"I wonder if that damned air-conditioning unit is acting up again," he said to Jason. "It doesn't feel any cooler in here than it did outside."

"DON'T TELL ME THE air-conditioning in this building is broken again." Annabelle slammed the office door behind her, thoroughly out of sorts. Hilda, the receptionist, gave her an astonished look over the top of her half-moon glasses.

Damn Ben Baxter, anyhow. The man had thrown her so completely that she'd been unable to do her job the way she usually could. He'd made her nervous, he'd thrown her off her stride, and even the forty-minute drive back to Kelowna hadn't been enough to get over the effect he'd had on her.

He'd refused to even glance at her offer.

A fan oscillated to and fro on a table, doing absolutely nothing to cool the stifling air.

One of her partners, Cyril Lisk, grinned at her from the open door of his office. Cyril was wearing khaki shorts, a wildly patterned Hawaiian shirt and his sandal-clad feet were propped up on his desk. It irritated Annabelle that he could look cool in the midst of such heat. He also could appear indolent even though he did an enormous amount of the work for their subsidiary company, Pinetree Developments, such as hiring of tradespeople and overseeing the construction of several projects.

Cyril had taught her most of what she knew about selling. Years older and more experienced than she, he'd taken her under his wing years before, after she'd passed the real-estate exam.

"You now know all the wherefores and howevers. What you need to learn is the art of gentle persuasion, the real art of selling," he'd told her. "Be clear about what you want and focus on it. Never accept failure, and know your client inside and out. And always look out for number one."

Cyril had been a good friend as well as a good teacher, although Annabelle had always regretted that she didn't get along with Cyril's wife, Madeline. Madeline was a social climber and a snob. She also suspected at times that the older woman was more than a little jealous of her. It puzzled her how a thoroughly nice man like Cyril could live with someone like Madeline.

Not that there was a thing to be jealous of in Annabelle and Cyril's relationship. They'd been nothing more than good partners over the years. Together, they'd built up a business selling residential real estate, and when they branched out into property development five years before, it was Cyril's background in construction that had benefited Pinetree Developments as much as Annabelle's ability to ferret out unlikely chunks of land and see their potential. They were a good team, along with Johnny Calvados, the third partner.

"I suppose you don't want to hear that our three tenants were all in to complain about the lack of cool air," Cyril said. "Johnny's on the phone this minute trying to get a repairman, which will be a small miracle at this time of the year."

The Okanagan was British Columbia's desert oasis, and temperatures stayed high from early spring to late fall.

"Why can't some smart woman invent an air-conditioning unit that works? You men have failed miserably at it." Annabelle stalked into her own office, where the westerly sun was doing its best to melt her bright red vertical blinds. She put her dirty, battered briefcase on the desktop and closed the blinds as tightly as they would go.

Even her silk ficus plant looked as if it was wilting, she decided with a sigh of utter dejection, sinking down into the cushioned softness of her leather desk chair—and feeling her thighs instantly glue themselves to the leather right through her silk trousers.

Cyril sauntered in and sat down in the matching chair. "The lack of a brass band tells me Mr. Baxter didn't break his fingers signing our offer on the cove."

"You got that right. I've never encountered a more positive negative in my life." She opened her briefcase and took out several bundles of paper, arranging them with deliberate precision on her desktop.

"Well, you know the rules," Cyril said. "Consider it just a detour on the road to success. Think positive, find out everything you can about him, and hammer away until you get what you want. Do whatever it takes. We've got until September, and I'm sure Baxter will come around. Everybody has a price."

"Right." Cyril's cynicism was annoying her today. She made a pretense of jabbing numbers into her calculator, and Cyril finally took the hint and ambled out. She wished she could slam her office door behind him, but without air-conditioning, she'd expire.

In a moment he was back, leaning on her door-frame, his thick white eyebrows raised questioningly. "By the by, what happened to your new briefcase? It looks as if it got run over by a truck."

"Two llamas and a dog," she snapped. "Look, Cyril, I'm not exactly feeling sociable here. Don't you have something else to do?"

"Llamas?" He gave a silent whistle, then waited for her to elaborate. When she didn't, he shrugged and wandered off again, and she felt ashamed of herself. Cyril and Johnny were her friends as well as her business partners, and there was no excuse for being rude.

The truth of the matter was, she was boiling hot, unnerved and totally off-balance from her meeting with Benjamin Baxter, and she felt utterly terrified into the bargain.

The terror was nothing new; it was becoming a constant companion as the deadline on the development deal drew closer. She managed to control her panic most of the time, but every mile back from Oyama today she'd been more and more convinced that she'd gotten the firm into an impossible situation this time, and that because of her abject failure with Ben Baxter, she'd never manage to extricate them in time.

The situation wasn't just impossible, she reflected, swinging her chair around and scowling at the map of the Okanagan Valley that covered one wall to the right of her desk. To be honest, the situation was ominous. She and her two partners were in grave danger of losing Midas Realty and Pinetree Developments, of having to declare bankruptcy unless . . .

Unless she could somehow talk the impossible Benjamin Baxter into selling Likely Cove to them before September. And she had the awful, sinking feeling that

Baxter had never been talked into anything in his entire life.

A noise at the door drew her attention away from the map. What looked like a broomstick with a piece of white paper toweling taped to it dangled in her doorway. It had Peace scrawled on it in huge black letters with a gigantic question mark underneath.

Johnny Calvados, holding the broom, stuck his head around the doorframe, a teasing grin on his handsome features. "Cy warned me it was like a war zone in here, so I figured I'd better test the atmosphere. Is there sniping going on?"

Annabelle couldn't help smiling back at him. "Peace, partner. Come in. I shouldn't have taken Cy's head off. It's not his fault I'm hot and cranky." She shook her head and gestured at the map. "It's this infernal thing about Likely Cove that has me steamed. This guy who owns it, this Benjamin Baxter, is . . . is . . ."

She paused, at a loss for words. How could she summarize her meeting with Ben Baxter so that anyone remotely sane could understand?

"Well, the best one could say is that he's like the immovable object and the irresistible force all rolled into one. He wouldn't even glance at our offer. He insists that nothing will ever tempt him to sell, and the worst part of it is, I believe him. The man doesn't seem to run on any system of logic I can figure out."

Johnny gave her a roguish wink. "C'mon, hotshot, where's that famous confidence? The man doesn't exist who won't eventually succumb to your subtle sales pitch. You're like water dripping on stone—you wear away resistance in the nicest possible way. Go see the guy again tomorrow. And the day after that, if that's what it takes."

How could she admit that she didn't want to see Ben Baxter again, preferably ever? There was something about the man that she found both disturbing and unsettling. He made her feel . . . at risk, somehow. Vulnerable. Young and ridiculously inexperienced.

She shook her head. "I'll try, but I think this is a hopeless case, Johnny."

"Am I really hearing this from you, the lady who never gives up?" He studied her face, and there must have been something in her expression that convinced him she meant what she said.

He shrugged and held his hands out, palms up. "Well, if this guy won't sell, then he won't. We'll just have to go back to the drawing board and search out a whole new set of investors, that's all."

"A new set of investors?" Annabelle rolled her eyes to the ceiling. "You're an incurable optimist if ever there was one."

Johnny Calvados was an optimist. He was also a lucky gambler and one hell of a salesman. She'd never been sorry that she'd pressured and nagged Cyril until he'd grudgingly agreed they should invite Johnny to join the firm four years before.

At that time, Johnny was taking the local real-estate market by storm and talking of setting up a firm of his own, and Cyril and Annabelle desperately needed a third agent—business was booming and they were rushed off their feet.

Johnny had driven a hard bargain. He'd put money into the company, but he'd also insisted on a healthy share in both Midas and Pinetree.

Cyril hadn't liked it at all, but as Annabelle had pointed out, better to have the likes of Johnny on their team than batting against them.

But there were times, like right now, when Annabelle felt that he wasn't as practical as he should be.

"For heaven's sake, Johnny, you know that finding new investors is not only improbable, it's hopeless."

Irritation was once again obvious in her voice. "The financial situation in North America isn't getting any better. We don't have much time here. The bank's going to get nervous unless they see some action with that property in the near future. I'm nervous myself. I don't have to tell you that Pinetree is seriously overextended—thanks to our mortgage on this darned piece of property. And with the softening of the residential market, Midas isn't in any position to make loans. Our cash flow is dismal at the moment."

Her eyes moved again to the map, drawn like magnets to the wedge-shaped chunk of land Pinetree had purchased along the northeast shore of ninety-mile-long Okanagan Lake—the "privately owned parcel" she'd mentioned to Ben Baxter. When it had come on the market last fall, it was one of the last large, choice tracts in the entire area. It had enormous development potential, and developers immediately began making offers.

Despite their reservations, Annabelle had convinced her partners Pinetree should buy it—regardless of the astronomical asking price. Their offer had been the high bid, and with the help of major bank financing, they'd snatched the parcel right from under the nose of their major competitor, Golden Circle Realty—which just happened to be owned by her ex-husband, Theodore Winslow. Theo had been furious, naturally, and she'd been elated.

Beating Theo at his own game had been the reason she'd gotten into real estate in the first place, and this particular victory was sweet.

The thrill of the coup quickly wore thin, however, when one setback followed another. Up till that point, their cash flow had been good, and the massive bank payments were possible because housing sales were phenomenal, and Midas could always loan money to Pinetree if necessary. *Had* loaned Pinetree a sizable amount over the years, in fact. Pinetree had been slow at showing profit, but as Cyril often reminded her, a development company was a long-range investment. When it started to pay off, it would pay off big.

But it seemed one disaster followed hard on the next. Housing sales took a downturn, and suddenly Midas, too, was in serious trouble. The bank hadn't as yet pressured them unduly, but Annabelle knew it was inevitable.

Any possibility of developing the new property themselves, as they'd originally planned, was now inconceivable. Annabelle and her partners hastily put together a prospectus for the development property, with plans for a lavish resort and golf course, which to their delighted relief attracted the interest of foreign investors.

Drawn by the valley's tourist potential, the desertlike heat and deep, cool lakes, plus the rugged beauty of the British Columbia landscape, a group of Chinese investors had agreed to finance the development.

And then . . . still another calamity. The worldwide economic climate went soft, and everybody got nervous before the papers were signed on the deal.

Annabelle's stomach tightened even now, as she remembered what happened next.

Last week, three of the investors had flown in by private jet—Mr. Sam, Mr. Wong and Mr. Tsui.

"We would like to view the development area again, if you please, before we make a final commitment." Mr. Sam, the low-key spokesman for the group, had smiled apologetically at Annabelle.

"But of course, I'd be delighted to take you out there this morning." She'd tacked her professional smile in place and borrowed Cyril's impressive black Cadillac sedan to drive them up the winding and less-than-perfect gravel road that led to the remote property, chatting pleasantly all the way about the wildlife in the area, the pleasures of boating on the lake, the wonderful climate of the Okanagan, and the potential for growth that was only beginning to be tapped.

Two of her passengers had talked fast and low in the back seat while Mr. Sam made polite chitchat with her. Then the three had spent hours walking over every inch of the property, asking the same questions again and again. She'd kept her smile in place and patiently answered everything, subtly stressing all the while the enormous profits to be made when the development was operational, the truly wonderful view of the nearby lake that the area afforded, and the scarcity of locations like this one in which to build resorts.

They'd walked at least fifty times down the steep incline to the lake and back up the hill to the property, and by the time she had them loaded in the car for the return trip, she'd felt as though she'd run a marathon, undergone brain surgery and been away at least a month.

"My partners and I insist that you join us for dinner," she'd purred as she dropped the three at their hotel. Apprehension had dogged her as she raced home to shower and change. There had been a lot of negative head shaking and what sounded like arguments to Annabelle.

She'd made reservations at one of Kelowna's best restaurants, and she'd done her best to be charming all during the meal, relating anecdotes of the real-estate business she thought their guests might find amusing. Nothing was said about the business proposition until they were all sipping liqueurs with their coffee.

By that time, Annabelle was completely exhausted and positive that the three gentlemen were about to ever-so-politely renege on the whole thing, leaving her and her partners in a financial position she couldn't bring herself to even contemplate.

Her heart was hammering and her hands felt clammy with apprehension when at last Mr. Sam had set down his glass, cleared his throat, and begun to speak.

"We are still very much interested in this resort concept," he'd said, and Annabelle had thought she'd faint with relief.

"However," he'd continued as she tensed up all over again, "there are conditions to our finalizing the agreement. We now feel that putting a road in to the property would be much too costly at this time. Water access is more practical, yes?"

Annabelle had wanted to scream no, but she'd bitten her tongue and kept an expression of rapt interest on her face.

"Your Okanagan Lake is ninety miles long. There is the dock right here in downtown Kelowna, and the property, although not lakefront, has a water view. Transporting clients by water is much less expensive than improving the existing road. And there is that small cove nearby that would be perfect for a dock."

Likely Cove, Annabelle's beleaguered brain had supplied. No wonder they'd walked her up and down the damned hillside all day from the property to Likely Cove and back. Well, they were correct in thinking Likely Cove would be perfect for a dock. It would be; the suggestion was practical enough. She'd felt a bit envious—she should have thought of it herself.

There was just one small problem.

"Our company doesn't own Likely Cove." Cyril was the one who'd told the three gentlemen that fact.

"Oh, we understand that, but surely," Mr. Sam had suggested with an encouraging smile, "a deal can be struck on such an otherwise-worthless, rocky piece of coastline? Without it, we would unfortunately have to look elsewhere for the purpose of investing. Please, there's no rush. Your company has until the first of September to think over our offer."

The computer in Annabelle's brain had ticked off figures. By September, even the interest on the bank loans would be astronomical. It was essential that a deal be struck now to show the bank.

So a document had been drawn up and duly signed, subject to the purchase of Likely Cove.

And now Ben Baxter had said an unequivocal no.

"Maybe we ought to just put the land back on the market," Johnny speculated, frowning at the map right along with Annabelle.

She sighed. The same idea had crossed her mind more than once during the past tense weeks, but that solution wouldn't work, either.

Johnny put into words what they both knew. "Too bad the price of land slipped this drastically. On today's market, we couldn't get two-thirds what we paid for the damn piece. We'd lose our shirts."

"We might be going to anyway." Annabelle cleared her throat. "This is basically all my fault, Johnny. I'm aware of that. You and Cy did make cautionary noises, and I didn't listen. I steamrollered you two into this, and I'll have to figure a way out, that's all."

Johnny, ever the gentleman, did his best to refute her claim of responsibility, but deep inside, she knew the truth.

For ten years, she'd tried her best to even the score with Theo, doggedly becoming a fast-talking real-estate agent—even though that persona was far from her natural personality—just so she could meet him on his own ground and maybe find a way to beat him at his own business. He'd hurt her so deeply she had to find a way to hurt him back—her pride demanded it.

Over the years, there'd been small triumphs, small victories that she knew had irked him. So when she heard how avidly Theo's company wanted the development property, she'd allowed her emotions to overshadow her good sense; and worst of all, she'd fast-talked her partners into going along with her.

"Well, as long as you're feeling this guilty, I might as well take advantage of you," Johnny said, winking one dark brown eye at her. "Tomorrow night's the monthly meeting of the Regional District, and I know I agreed to go but Gillian's in a school play and I promised I'd be there. Caroline can't make it, she's got personal-growth classes or something—as usual."

Johnny had recently gone through a bitter and costly divorce from Caroline, and was trying hard to get custody of his eight-year-old daughter.

"Any chance you could fill in for me, Annabelle?" His tone was coaxing. "I already asked Cy but it's Madeline's birthday and he's taking her out for dinner. This meeting's important. They're going to discuss our petition for rezoning that chunk of land Bellamy wants out in the Mission. We get a sure sale if the rezoning goes through—Bellamy's going to build town houses."

Meetings of the Regional District were important to the firm. They provided insider information on subjects like this proposed rezoning and other land issues that could be important to them.

"Johnny, this is the third time in a month I've filled in for you at some meeting or other," Annabelle replied with a sharp edge in her voice. She thought longingly of the outdoor pool at her apartment, and the leisurely swim in the cool water that she looked forward to every day. She had a new mystery novel she hadn't had a chance to even open, and tonight she desperately had to go grocery shopping.

She was the only one of the three without family responsibilities, and often found herself filling in for Johnny or Cy at events like tonight's meeting. It bothered the hell out of her. Somehow, both men had come to assume that her leisure time was less important than theirs, simply because she was without family.

The worst part of all was that she couldn't even plead a heavy social schedule. Since her divorce from Theo all those years ago, she'd avoided men who wanted intensity or commitment or passion in their relationships with her, which narrowed the field considerably.

Eliminated it, if she was being bone honest here, she thought with bitter humor. She had a few female friends—career women like herself—but apart from hurried lunches or the odd weekend dinner, they didn't see much of one another. Her friends seemed to date more than she did, and two of them now had live-in partners.

It had been— She added the weeks in her head. Could it really have been over three months since she'd been out on anything remotely resembling a date?

Suddenly the specter of living all the years of her life alone overwhelmed her, and a feeling of emptiness made her shiver despite the heat.

Maybe, she thought in a wry effort to shake herself out of the doldrums, she ought to bow to the inevitable and get herself a cat—except that her building didn't allow pets.

She blew out an exasperated breath before she said reluctantly, "Okay, I'll go. But you owe me."

Johnny beamed at her and reached over to give her shoulder a friendly thump. "Thanks, Annabelle. You're a trooper."

She didn't feel much like a trooper the following evening as she slipped into the meeting room at the Regional District offices and found a seat near the front. She just felt frozen.

The room was like a small amphitheater, with staggered wooden seats for visitors and a long, low table front and center for the elected representatives from the various districts, and she'd forgotten they kept it air-conditioned to within an inch of the icicle stage. The contrast between the intense heat outside and the chill indoors was enough to cause pneumonia.

She'd worn a cool linen sundress in a cheerful lemon yellow, and she felt goose bumps break out on her bare arms. She huddled down into her seat and wondered if it was possible to get frostbite in Kelowna in July.

Someone with warm, callused fingers touched her shoulder and she jumped.

"Why don't you wear this? I'm used to the temperature in here." He leaned close to her ear and whispered, "I wore long underwear so I won't be needing my jacket."

Annabelle gaped up at Ben Baxter—a Ben Baxter she barely recognized. He was clean-shaven, apart from his well-trimmed mustache, sober, and strikingly handsome in a crisp blue striped cotton shirt and lightweight gray trousers.

Her heart gave a funny lurch as he draped a black leather motorcycle jacket around her shoulders, grinned widely, then winked with one of his inordinately blue eyes. He moved with lithe grace down to the front to take his seat with the representatives of the Regional District before she could gather her wits and close her mouth enough to say a single word.

# 3

BEN SAT AT ONE SIDE of the table. When the meeting was called to order, he looked in her direction and smiled. She felt flustered and flattered all at the same time.

"If the secretary will read the minutes of the last meeting . . ."

Gradually, as the first half-hour passed, she adjusted to the idea of Ben Baxter as Oyama's regional representative, although she told herself that Oyama mustn't have a wide field of suitable applicants to choose from, if all they could come up with was an RCMP dropout who grew grapes, kept strange animals as pets and drank too much.

She looked at him and remembered those disgraceful blue-jean shorts and what they hadn't covered. She found herself speculating on whether or not he was wearing some of the skimpy black or red underwear she'd glimpsed in his bathroom.

Feeling more than a little wicked and slightly guilty at the way her mind was working, she snuggled into the welcoming warmth of his leather jacket. It was well-worn; the leather was soft and supple. It smelled of him—a woodsy, subtle odor that made her think of balmy evenings and dusty country roads. There was something solid and sturdy about Ben Baxter's jacket . . . an impression that she had to admit Ben himself gave at this moment, sitting down there with six other regional representatives.

Annabelle awarded each of them an impartial but thorough eyeballing, and had to conclude that Ben was the only one with anything remotely resembling sex appeal. In fact, he was the best-looking man at the table.

Most of the others had potbellies and balding heads, except for the one woman rep. She had plenty of hair but she looked formidable, in walking shorts and knee socks, with a no-nonsense white shirt and straight salt-and-pepper hair held back with a plastic headband.

The meeting was tedious. There was an endless discussion about the shocking condition of isolated areas in Winfield, a small village situated between Kelowna and Oyama, due to unlawful garbage dumping. Annabelle's mind drifted, and she found herself speculating on the women in Ben Baxter's life.

There had to be women, considering the blatant sex appeal he exuded like some heavy cologne. Were his women mindless young bimbos charmed by his carefree life-style and startling good looks? Or were they older, more worldly, more . . . sophisticated in their tastes?

For heaven's sake, what possible difference could it make to her what type of woman he preferred? What was wrong with her, to be thinking about him like this?

She forced herself to pay attention to what was going on. The group around the table was now involved in a long harangue concerning the advisability of another stoplight in Winfield, and that was followed by a boring discourse on sewers.

Had he ridden his motorcycle to the meeting? She wondered what it felt like, swooping along the highway on a motorbike. Reckless, windblown, carefree? The only time in her entire life she'd experienced those reactions was when she'd first met Theo in Greece, and had fallen in love with him.

And look where that had landed her.

The issue of zoning that interested Annabelle was introduced and she sat up straight and paid attention. The motion to change the zoning from single-family dwellings to multiple units was discussed and then passed without any real opposition.

She could go home now if she wanted to. She started to get up.

"I'd like to bring up the matter of deer in the orchards of Oyama," Ben was saying, and Annabelle sank down again onto the hard wooden chair.

Deer? In the orchards?

"Orchardists are concerned that the animals are eating the tender new leaves and the undeveloped fruit, thus damaging the crops. There's a petition being circulated for an open hunting season that concerns me. This would allow not only the residents of Oyama to shoot these pesky deer, but it would also attract hunters from far and wide eager to bag their limit without having to work their butts off climbing mountains and falling in rivers."

The air of boredom that had permeated the room seemed to dissolve with Ben's easy delivery. With the lift of an eyebrow, a tone of voice that emphasized the irony of his words, he captured his audience and held them.

Annabelle listened, and her notions about Ben Baxter began to shift and change. This was an impressive man, able to present his point of view in a clear, concise and relaxed manner. He even made his audience laugh now and then, which certainly hadn't happened with any speaker before him.

"I have a small orchard myself," he was saying, "and I understand the concerns of my neighbors. I've had an entire family of freeloading, irresponsible, jobless deer camped on my property since early spring, and believe me, I'd like to evict them."

Annabelle laughed with the others.

"But not with guns, ladies and gentlemen. I have to admit I feel a certain amount of anxiety at the idea of armed men or women creeping through the orchards at dawn, firing away at anything that moves. What we need to address here is the amazing number of domestic cattle that are mistaken for wild animals every hunting season. In Oyama, we have our fair share of cattle, goats, llamas, horses and even eccentrics like myself who occasionally wander through orchards at dawn, happy but more or less comatose. Meeting Rambo with a deer tag he wants to pin to my ear isn't exactly my idea of a good time."

Annabelle was fascinated by his facility with words. His voice was pleasing—a deep, soft bass. She'd missed noticing his voice the day before, which was understandable, given his seminude state and his hung-over condition.

Both were gone tonight. Tonight he was smooth and articulate, with an air of straightforward honesty that impressed her.

He suggested putting up fences as an alternative to shooting, or, he added, one could simply own a dog who'd chase the deer off.

"And of course," he concluded with a forthright grin, "we could always just share a little. The deer were in the valley long before us, and in my experience, they don't eat all that much."

Everyone was smiling when he finished, and the entire group voted against extending the hunting season.

The meeting broke up shortly after that, and Annabelle waited in her seat as Ben shook hands and exchanged greetings with several people he knew. She watched him, noting the easy grin that came and went frequently, the warmth and humor and energy that seemed to draw people to him.

She'd seriously misjudged Ben Baxter. The contradictions between the man she'd met the day before and the man she'd seen in action tonight both puzzled and confused her. The half-naked eccentric of yesterday had been difficult enough to contend with, but tonight's glimpse of a forthright diplomat who swayed people with his humor and his glib tongue totally unnerved her.

She didn't quite know what to do now. She didn't want to rush down to the front, hand him his jacket, and have to be introduced to his friends, but she felt it would be rude to just leave his jacket on the chair without thanking him. She found herself getting more and more tense as the moments dragged by and most of the other people in the room made a fast exit.

At last, he broke away, and came over to her.

"I was hoping you'd wait." There was a vibrancy about him that seemed to reach out and envelop her. The top buttons of his shirt were open, and she couldn't help but remember how his chest looked bare.

She got to her feet and held out his jacket, feeling awkward. "Thank you very much for this. I'd have frozen without it. Why on earth do they keep it so cold in here?"

He grinned—a wide, crooked grin that was somehow slightly wicked. "To keep people from going to sleep, of course. These meetings aren't exactly riveting, as I'm sure you noticed." He accepted the jacket and took her arm in a courteous gesture, walking beside her to the exit.

The air outside was balmy. It was a typical midsummer Kelowna night. Beyond the streetlights, out over the nearby lake, shone an indecent-size moon flanked by acres of stars. After the frigid meeting room, the warmth was glorious.

Annabelle had left her car in the nearby lot, and Ben stayed at her side until she reached it.

"Well, thanks again for your jacket," she said, fumbling in her purse for her keys, all too aware of his body far too close to hers. Where were the damn keys, anyhow?

"Look, it's early, barely nine-thirty. Would you consider having a glass of wine with me? Or coffee, or juice. Whatever you like."

Could it be hesitancy she heard in his tone?

"I wasn't exactly at my best yesterday at the trailer. I had the worst hangover of my entire adult life and I'm afraid I was somewhat less than amiable. Give me a chance to correct that bad first impression, okay, Annabelle?"

She knew he found her attractive—women always knew things like that. She'd been half expecting he'd suggest a drink, and she had a gracious refusal all planned. But perversely, now that the moment had arrived, she found herself wanting to say yes.

It was a beautiful night, still early. The trouble was, she hated bars and cocktail lounges—the smoke and the noise and the atmosphere—and coffee kept her awake. She told him so.

"No problem. We'll go down to the beach and have a glass of wine." That intriguing grin came and went, his teeth flashing very white in the dusk. "You know where *The Sails* are, by the park?"

She did, of course. The sculpture of *The Sails* was a landmark, set in downtown Kelowna on the edge of the park that bordered the lake.

"Drive down there and wait for me. I'll be ten or fifteen minutes. My bike's right over there." He gestured at a motorcycle, parked on the other side of her car.

She hesitated. What kind of madness was it to agree to meet an almost stranger alone on the beach? But tonight there'd be dozens of other people out as well, she assured herself. It would be anything but isolated. And she'd sat for a good hour alone with him in his trailer, when he'd been wearing a lot less clothing than now, and nothing obscene had happened.

Unless you counted his refusal of her offer.

But there was that prickly awareness he aroused in her.

There was also Likely Cove, and the opportunity to talk to him, establish some sort of rapport that might make him more receptive to her sales pitch. Deals in real estate, as Cy had always told her, were mostly a mixture of hot air, greed and bravado, and she'd struck out on all counts with Ben Baxter.

"Trust me, Annabelle?"

Of course, she didn't. Not one whit. A woman would have to be demented to trust a man with a smile like his, with that deep, compelling voice.

Then she thought of Likely Cove and how much she needed his signature on a sales agreement. It couldn't hurt to get to know him a little better, perhaps find some way to convince him to sell the cove. After all, as he'd just admitted, he hadn't exactly been in a receptive mood yesterday.

She finally found her keys. He took them from her and opened her car door. She climbed in, trying to keep her skirt from sliding up over her thighs, and failing. It was a problem in these small, low cars.

"What d'you say?" He had one hand on her door. The other held the jacket slung over one shoulder. He wasn't ogling her legs, yet she knew she had rather good legs. She felt a little disappointed, and then amused at herself.

"Very well, then. Fifteen minutes."

He snapped off a military salute, making her smile as he closed the door and hurried over to his motorcycle.

She heard the low, guttural roar of its motor catching as she drove away.

HE PARKED BETWEEN TWO cars in front of The Finer Choice, a local restaurant whose proprietor had shared many a bottle of wine and good conversation with him. He sat for a moment before going in.

Why was he going to all this trouble to charm this particular woman? She was attractive, but not drop-dead beautiful. She was involved in a profession noted for cutthroat tactics and hard, cold materialism—traits that didn't appeal to him at all.

He tugged his helmet off and slid off the bike.

She was mysterious. He'd never been able to resist a mystery, and there was a mystery about Annabelle Murdoch. The professional charm and smooth conversation that were part and parcel of her working persona disappeared at the oddest times, allowing him to glimpse a different woman altogether. There ought to be a hardness that came with her profession. But it wasn't there.

So who was the woman behind the mask? Ben Baxter intended to find out tonight.

Grinning at his own sense of drama, he strode into the restaurant.

In less than five minutes he came out again, carefully stowed his packages in the saddlebags, and roared off, hoping against hope that Annabelle would do as she'd said and wait for him by *The Sails*.

He'd been surprised tonight when he'd driven into the parking lot of the Regional Offices and seen her car. He'd seriously thought about not coming to the damned meeting—Amos and Jacob were going fishing, and they'd wanted him to come along with them. But seeing they were the ones who'd been responsible for getting him elected regional rep in the first place, he reminded them nobly that he was obligated to attend the bloody meetings.

"See how jokes have a way of backfiring?" he gibed them. But the two had just laughed uproariously and borrowed some of his best tackle.

And now he had a feeling this was going to turn out way better than fishing, which he'd make a point of telling them tomorrow.

Provided, of course, Annabelle Murdoch's little red car was parked somewhere near *The Sails*, waiting for him.

He leaned over his handlebars and exceeded the speed limit, rounding the corner onto Bernard and focusing on the angled parking near the sculpture.

She wasn't there, God damn it to hell. He felt ridiculously disappointed, and some of the shine went out of the evening. He'd really wanted to spend some time with her.

Then he made a jubilant noise as he spotted her car, across the street and half a block away.

With a flourish, he pulled into the narrow space beside her and took off his helmet, running a hand through his hair.

She was sitting in her car, windows down, with soft music playing on the radio. Silk FM, he identified. Whatever happened to good old rock and roll?

He squatted down on his haunches and smiled in at her.

"Hi. Hope I'm not late." She seemed a bit apprehensive, but she smiled back at him and shook her head. "Fourteen minutes and thirty seconds," she assured him, and then blushed a little at revealing that she'd watched the time.

She looked pretty, her thick dark red cap of hair stylishly messed, her soft chocolate eyes shining in the dim light from the streetlamp. She'd put some fresh coral lipstick on, he noted. He could smell her perfume, sweet and light, mixing with the new-leather smell of the car's interior.

"Want to walk?"

She nodded.

He retrieved his packages from the saddlebags of the bike and led the way to one of the paths in City Park. Other couples were strolling there, enjoying the breathtaking view of the wide, dark lake, silvered by moonlight and backed by purple banks of mountain.

The sound of water lapping gently on the shore mingled with music from a nearby restaurant.

An isolated bench facing the lake was empty, and Ben gestured toward it. Annabelle sat, smoothing her yellow skirt down over what he'd noticed earlier were magnificent legs. She had a beautiful profile in the moonlight—a straight, aristocratic nose, a full mouth, a determined, well-defined chin. And that long, graceful neck.

He unwrapped the wine and, more cautiously, the long-stemmed glasses, balancing them on the bench. He dug in his pocket for his knife and, with an expert twist, popped the cork and poured, handing her a glass.

"I can't believe you managed real glasses. You went to a great deal of trouble." She sipped at the wine. "It's good wine, too."

He took a mouthful and considered. "It *is* good. Not as good as mine, but fine tasting all the same."

She smiled at him. "You're just a trifle arrogant about this wine you make, aren't you?" Her voice was faintly teasing.

"Not arrogant, or conceited, either." He shook his head. "Proud, yes. And honest. Being able to make the same fine wine my grandfather made gives me a great sense of accomplishment. I've always thought it stupid not to acknowledge what we do well. God knows, there's enough other things about ourselves to criticize, we might as well admit it when we're good at something."

She'd never thought about patting herself on the back for accomplishments. She'd always downplayed her talents and emphasized her weak spots, waiting for others to praise her. Ben's way had just never occurred to her.

He settled comfortably beside her, stretching his long legs out and crossing his ankles, turning a bit so he could look at her.

"You're very pretty, Annabelle."

It was a matter-of-fact statement, devoid of flattery, the way he said it. And it made her feel nice inside. She took a long swallow of wine, and it tasted cool and refreshing. "Thank you," she said. She'd read somewhere that the best possible response to a compliment was a simple thank-you.

"You go boating much on the lake?" he asked next, topping off her glass along with his own.

She shook her head. "I've only been out on the lake twice in all the years I've lived here. I don't own a boat, and even if I did, there wouldn't be much time to use it. In real estate, you tend to work most weekends."

"I know what you mean. Police work was the same— no respecter of ordinary days off."

"Is that why you retired so young?"

His white teeth flashed in the moonlight as he smiled at her. "Not so young as all that. I'm forty-four. And I told you the truth about why I retired. I wanted to try being a free spirit for at least part of my life."

He had told her that, but she'd figured he was joking with her. Now she wasn't so sure.

"And are you enjoying it? Don't you ever feel..." She hesitated, not sure how to phrase what she'd been about to say. He rescued her.

"Lazy? Unproductive? Frivolous?" He chuckled, deep and low in his throat, and she was glad of the darkness. She was blushing, because those were the exact things she'd wanted to ask about.

"I don't feel any of that, not in the slightest. See, I did a heck of a lot of thinking, nights when I was on stake-out for some dumb drug bust, or days spent in meetings twice as boring as that one tonight."

His voice was serious, low and intimate.

She'd forgotten all about deliberately drawing him out. She was captivated, completely absorbed in what he was telling her. There was a naked honesty in his words that was compelling.

"I came to the conclusion that all that career-ladder climbing didn't mean beans to me. I figured out that when I got old, I didn't want to be sorry for all the things I'd wanted to do and never tried."

That struck a sensitive chord in her. How often had she told herself that someday, some magic day far off in the future, she'd get around to doing all the things she dreamed about?

"Well, being superintendent of the RCMP wasn't one of my deepest ambitions, believe me," he added with a laugh. "So as near as possible, I figured out what I did want and how to get it. It might have taken me a lot longer to be able to afford to retire, but I got lucky. Some mining stock I bought from a friend paid off big, and I took that as a sign. I quit the force the day I found out, and I've never regretted it once."

Yesterday, she'd thought he was the most irresponsible man she'd ever met. Tonight, he made more sense than most men she knew. She was used to men who bravely related tales of failed marriages, of lost opportunities, of broken dreams. And yet here was a man of—she had to smile to herself—a certain age, who professed to be perfectly happy with his life and times.

They sat in companionable silence for a while, sipping wine and soaking up the quiet night around them. At last, he turned to her and said coaxingly, "Now, Annabelle Murdoch from England, you know all about how I became a dropout in mid-life. How about telling me a little about you, how you ended up emigrating to Kelowna and selling real estate, for instance?"

Despite the wine and the moonlight, and the intimacy that had sprung up between them, old barriers clanged shut at his words. There were things too painful to talk about casually; too humiliating even now for her to confide in just anyone.

She glanced at him and then looked away, out over the lake, wishing it didn't have to be so. It would be a relief to talk freely, to tell Ben the true story and in the telling, forget about it.

She took another drink of her wine and knew that it couldn't be.

Reticence, the old habit of bitterness and the need for revenge forbade it. Feeling like a fraud, she resorted to the glib version she'd recited so many times over the years.

4

"I FINISHED MY SCHOOLING in England, went on a holiday to Greece, got married there and came to Canada with my husband. He was a Canadian."

She sensed the slight change in her voice, the flatness of tone when she mentioned Theo. She hurried on, aware that the man beside her was listening intently.

"Irreconcilable differences arose, as the lawyers say." She smiled a little, and realized with no sense of alarm that she was slightly drunk on the wine. It didn't matter; she'd perfected the story so she could have recited it standing on her head, sound asleep.

"We subsequently divorced, and I had to support myself somehow, so I chose real estate. After several years of working for someone else, I set up my own company, eventually took two partners, and lived happily ever after." She caught herself, too late. Had he picked up on the acidity of her tone? "End of story," she added hastily, tipping her glass up to her lips and swallowing in a reckless gesture.

She knew the story sounded as if she'd left an entire chapter out. She waited a little nervously to hear what he'd say next.

"No kids, Annabelle? You never considered remarriage? No 'significant others' along the way?"

She wasn't about to bare her soul, regardless of the wine, or the moonlight, or the inescapable charm of the man beside her.

But unexpectedly her chest ached, and she felt as if she might be going to cry. She fought against it, panicked at her loss of control. Why should his gentle probing touch such a depth of feeling in her? How could he so unerringly pinpoint all the things that she knew were missing from her life?

"No. None of the above," she replied, her tone harsh. She had to change the subject, put the focus back on him, or she was in serious danger of making a fool of herself.

She cleared her throat. "What about you, Ben? No children, no remarriage, no significant others?"

"No kids." She noticed that he'd avoided the rest of her question.

"My ex-wife didn't want kids." There was a wistfulness in his voice that touched her.

"Did you?" She realized how probing her questions had become and how reluctant she'd been about answering his, and she touched his arm before he could respond and apologized. "Sorry. I'm being far too personal."

He reached up and covered her hand with his own, holding it in place on his arm for a long moment. His skin was warm and dusted with soft hair, and her palm tingled with the contact.

"Hell, I don't mind you asking questions. The fact is, I wanted a houseful of kids. It's one of the few things in my life I regret—never having children."

She was silent for several long moments, and they sipped their wine companionably.

"Me too," she said abruptly, surprising herself. "I always wanted children. I still do, as a matter of fact." Her voice was so soft, she wondered if he'd heard her. "I've never been tempted to marry again, but I've given a lot of thought to having a child."

Ben made a sympathetic sound. "It can be real hard on a kid, though, having just one parent." Then, as though he thought maybe she'd figure he was being judgmental or something, he hastily added, "Not that I think it's wrong or anything. I just know a kid who lives alone with his mom, and he has a few problems because of it. You met him yesterday. Jason. But you can't generalize about situations. Each one's different, and lots of kids make out just fine with a single parent." He sounded a little too hearty, as though he was trying to persuade himself as well as her.

It wasn't anything she hadn't thought of plenty of times. "I gave it lots of consideration and decided against it for myself."

She was amazed at what she was confiding, after she'd determined not to. It had to be the wine. "At least for the time being, anyway. My job takes a great deal of time and energy, and I don't think that would be fair to a child. However, there's also the fact that I'm getting older, and having a baby becomes less and less feasible with each year that passes."

So many dreams had shriveled and died over the years. A fierce longing seized her. Why had she never pursued happiness the way Ben seemed to have done? With a flash of clarity, she admitted to herself that even her job didn't give her the satisfaction it once had.

She forced her mind away from painful things, concentrating instead on the pleasant physical sensation of sitting here on this lovely summer night, beside a handsome man.

She was conscious of his thigh, inches away from her own. He was such a large man, but he was also in great physical condition. Out of the corner of her eye, she could see the muscles in his arms, bared by the short-sleeved shirt. She liked the way his arms looked. How would they feel around her?

God. The wine was making her careless, yet she didn't mind too much. She allowed herself to fantasize about being in his arms, the way her breasts would feel pressed close to his chest. Her breath quickened and her body grew warm and heavy.

She knew what that chest looked like, that mat of thick curls, the beautifully developed shoulders. She swallowed hard and tried to concentrate on what he was saying.

"Do you like real estate, Annabelle? Is it something you can't wait to get up in the morning and go off and do?"

She considered the best way of answering that, and he refilled her wineglass during the pause. The truth was, during the past months there had been too many days when she'd hated what she did for a living; hated the stress, the scrabbling for listings, the constant worrying over money. But she couldn't reveal that to him, either. Why were there so many things in her life she couldn't be honest about? She hated deceitful people, but somehow she'd become one herself. She chose her words carefully.

"I find my job challenging, and most of the time I enjoy it. There are times when it can get a bit stressful." That was the understatement of the year. She thought of the bank and shuddered.

He must have thought she was chilly, because he looped his arm around her shoulders and gave her a little squeeze. Having him touch her made every nerve ending spring to disturbing life, and she considered moving away, but not seriously. She gave in to the comfort and security his strength seemed to provide, the thrill of having his bare arm touching her bare shoulders, his side pressed to hers.

There was a catch in her voice when she went on with what she had to say, though. "As for getting up in the morning, I'm not a morning person at all."

A vivid memory of him standing in the trailer doorway, half naked and scowling out at her, made her add recklessly, "Although I have to say I'm not as desperately bad at mornings as you seem to be." A traitorous little giggle escaped her, and she knew she'd had far too much wine. It was making her lose all her inhibitions.

"You're a proper ogre when you first get up, Ben. You scared me half to death yesterday when you burst out that door shouting at poor Jason." She laughed outright.

There was a hint of laughter in his voice, too. "C'mon now, you can't judge a man on one unfortunate episode, can you? I apologize for all that. Yesterday wasn't normal for me at all. That's the first time I've been hung over in . . ." He paused, ignoring the disbelieving look she was giving him. He apparently wanted her to be clear on the fact that he wasn't a problem drinker. He was so terribly sincere about it all that she felt a pang of tenderness for him.

"Hell, I'll bet it's been three or four years since the last time I came close to drinking that much."

She looked at him for a long, considering moment. It seemed the right time to bring up the matter of the cove, but for some strange reason she hated doing it.

"Have you had a chance to think about the offer I left on the coffee table?"

He was surprised she'd ask again...and maybe a little disappointed as well, judging by the expression on his face. And Ben's face was a reflection of what he was thinking, she realized.

His answer was abrupt. "No. I didn't read it because as I told you, it's totally out of the question."

She didn't respond to that at all. His arm was still around her shoulders, but she could feel the tension in his muscles.

"Is that why you agreed to have a glass of wine with me tonight, Annabelle?" He sounded betrayed, and she felt terrible.

She didn't deny it, however. There was something about Ben that seemed to demand she be as honest as she could be.

Within reason, of course.

She looked straight into his eyes and said in a level tone, "Partially, yes. I suppose I was hoping."

Her honesty brought a wry smile to his lips. "And here I thought you were overcome by my fatal charm. Now I see it's only my land you're after." He shook his head in mock chagrin and moaned, "Why can't it be my sexy body?"

"You *are* sexy, Ben." Good grief, the wine was making her say things she'd never dream of saying, sober. Well, in for a penny... She threw caution to the winds. "I'm sure you're a great success with women. There aren't that many eligible bachelors around this area, especially ones over thirty."

He threw back his head and laughed—a wonderful, deep-throated sound that delighted her.

Well, if he thought it was funny, she might as well keep right on probing. Her curiosity totally overcame her good manners. "Have you had a lot of practice? Captivating females?"

He wasn't at all uncomfortable. He wasn't even teasing. His voice was thoughtful instead, and again, he seemed to be telling the truth. "I've had my fair share, no question. Right now, there isn't any particular woman I'm involved with. How about you, Annabelle? I can't believe there aren't dozens of men courting you. You're a beautiful woman."

He reached out and ran a rough forefinger slowly down the softness of her cheek, stopping just short of her lips. A deep, lethargic warmth spread into her abdomen, and a danger sign flashed loud and clear in her mind.

"Is all this beauty being wasted on the desert air?" His voice was husky and resonant, and she could feel her heartbeat accelerate and every nerve ending come alive at his touch.

"I'm—" her voice was strained "—I'm the same as you. Plenty of friends, but that's as far as it goes. I told you before, I've never had any desire to get seriously involved again. The men I see understand and respect that."

He snorted, and she jumped a little. "Those men must be total idiots." He actually sounded amazed and a little angry. "I'd never settle for anything less than passion with you, Annabelle."

In spite of herself, his audacious words thrilled her. They were so impossibly, ridiculously romantic. They were so exactly what she wanted . . . needed . . . to hear at this particular moment.

He took the glass she was still holding out of her nerveless fingers and set it down on the bench beside his own, and she knew he was about to kiss her. Her heart started to hammer against her ribs until she could hardly breathe, and she spent a panicked half second wondering what she ought to do, but by the time she'd decided she really ought to move away, he had her in his arms.

He was incredibly sure of himself. He drew her close and put a hand on the back of her head, urging her toward him. His lips teased over hers, tender and undemanding, giving her plenty of time to get used to the feeling, lulling her into thinking that this would be just another companionable, gentle kiss—something a trifle more than a hug between friends, but nothing extraordinary. His mustache intrigued her. She'd never kissed anyone with a mustache before. It was soft and prickly at the same time. It was indescribably sensual.

Just as she relaxed that smallest bit, he unleashed what she could only describe afterward as raw, unadulterated passion. He cradled her head in both hands this time and invaded her mouth, his lips hard and supple by turn, tender and then all at once ruthlessly demanding.

Her lips opened for him, and his tongue explored hers. It was as if he touched other, more hidden parts of her, touched them with intimate understanding of what pleased and incensed. Her body grew soft and pliant in his embrace, and her breasts felt swollen and needy. Her senses were captivated by the feel of him, his clean man smell, reminiscent of leather and soap, and the sensation of power his large body exuded like after-shave. His hands stroked her arms, her back, then cradled her head again. The kiss seemed to go on forever, and when at last it ended, she was trembling.

"Annabelle." He whispered her name close to her ear, and he made it sound like music. His hand slid down her shoulder, coming to rest dangerously near her breast. The heat of his skin burned through her thin dress.

"Lovely Annabelle."

*This isn't exactly the textbook method for persuading a client to part with valuable real estate, Annabelle Murdoch.*

She felt cheap, all of a sudden. She straightened her skirt and sat upright, brushing a hand through her hair, trying to draw a deep breath into her lungs and not quite succeeding. She didn't want to look at him or acknowledge the passion he'd stirred in her. She wanted to ignore the kiss, go back to just talking with him; it was a heck of a lot safer that way.

She should have known that Ben Baxter wouldn't let her do that.

"See, I was right about us," he said with maddening, self-satisfied confidence, letting his hand trail across her shoulder, stroking the bare skin around the straps of her sundress, unsettling her all over again.

"I knew it would be like holding a torch to kindling when we kissed."

"For heaven's sake, Ben, you couldn't have known anything of the kind." She sounded snappish because his fingers were causing new, disquieting sensations all up and down her arm; and the fact that she was responding despite herself bothered her beyond measure.

"Stop that." She removed his fingers, but he captured her hand in his and held it, touching her palm with his thumb, slipping his fingers between hers, then bringing her hand up to his lips and doing indecent things she'd never dreamed a person could do with only a hand to work with.

In desperation, she struggled to her feet. "Let's walk. I ought to be getting back to my car. It's getting late." She squinted at her watch, but its hands were too small to decipher in the moonlight.

He got up, towering over her, and with gentle insistence reclaimed the hand she'd yanked away. "Sure, let's walk. Good idea." He started to amble away, tugging her along with him.

"Are you just going to leave the wineglasses there? Someone's sure to come along and take them. There're a lot of vagrants in this park."

He smiled down at her. "We enjoyed them. Let's hope whoever finds them does, too. Didn't you see the sign in the park? It said, Practice Random Kindness And Senseless Acts Of Beauty."

"I didn't see any such sign. You just made that up."

"Well, if there isn't one posted, there ought to be, don't you think?"

She was feeling mulish. "It's pretty idealistic, if you ask me. Are you always this cavalier about your possessions?" She felt irritated with him and on edge. She steered them back toward the street where her car was parked.

"Depends on what it is. I don't get bent out of shape over stuff like two wineglasses. I'd probably get hot under the collar if somebody boosted my motorcycle, though. But generally, I try not to let things own me."

"That's not quite true, is it?" The words were out before she could stop them. "You won't even consider selling a piece of land that you have no intention of doing anything with. That's letting possessions own you, in my opinion."

He stopped abruptly, and because he still had her hand firmly in his, she was forced to stop, as well. She

looked up at him with trepidation. She already knew
he had a temper.

"I'm against the pattern development is taking in this
valley, Annabelle." His voice was quiet, but she could
sense the anger beneath the surface. "I didn't ask what
someone wants that cove for, because I know it must
have to do with developing the huge tract of land behind it, and I'd like to prevent that, if possible."

"That's ridiculous," she countered. "The area is ripe
for development. What harm can come of it? It pro-
motes industry, jobs, tourism . . ."

He was scowling down at her, and part of her knew
she was going about this all wrong. She was allowing
emotion to overrule her good sense. But he could be so
exasperating.

He didn't respond for a moment, and she could see
him struggling for control, just as she was. When he
spoke again his tone was quiet, but there was an undercurrent of steel in it.

"Annabelle, don't get me wrong here. I'm not a rav-
ing fanatic who thinks any type of growth is bad, but
what we're seeing in the Okanagan is development
without much thought about the eventual effect on our
environment. Sooner or later, our lakes, which are our
water supply, will diminish. Our climate will change as
more orchards are cut down to make room for houses.
We need to address these issues now, before they get to
be problems. Don't you think so?"

Before she could respond, he exhaled and added
softly, persuasively, "Anyway, this isn't a discussion we
ought to be having out here on a glorious night with the
stars shining all around us. Let's save it for a blustery
day when we haven't got much else to do but argue."

She had to agree with him; it was senseless to stand here and holler at one another. And she wasn't going to get anywhere with him by losing her temper, she knew that. But there was something about him that had the power to infuriate her, that was certain.

"Let me take you out to Likely Cove this weekend, and we'll sail the boat across to Paradise Island. I'll show you why it's special to me, and you can explain in detail why it's a good idea for me to sell the cove. Then I promise I'll listen to your point of view. We'll talk about all this rationally. Okay, Annabelle?"

It wasn't okay at all. She didn't want to ever have to see him again, she told herself. He was upsetting and bullheaded and smug and stubborn and utterly impossible.

And he kissed as if he'd personally invented the whole reproductive process, and she didn't want to have to deal with the traitorous part of herself that responded to those kisses.

But unless she could convince him to sell her Likely Cove, Midas Realty, the company she'd worked herself to the bone to establish, might just crumble.

She was hoist with her own petard—or was it Ben Baxter's, damn his charming hide?

"All right." She knew she sounded grumpy and grudging, and she didn't give a damn. "All right, you win."

He either didn't realize how out of sorts she was, or he didn't care. "That's fantastic. It'll be a great day, you'll see. I'll pick you up at eight Saturday morning."

He sounded elated, which vexed her even more.

"Sunday, at ten. I work, remember? And there're things I have to do Saturday."

"Ten on Sunday, then. No problem. We'll go out for breakfast—I know this place that makes killer breakfasts. What's your address?"

There was nothing to do except tell him. She rattled it off fast and he repeated it exactly.

They'd reached her car. She fumbled around in her bag, finding her keys, and when she did he took them from her and opened the door. She slid in and before she knew what he was going to do, he'd leaned down and kissed her, fast and hard, full on the lips.

"Thanks for a great evening, Annabelle. See you Sunday." He stood back on the curb and waited for her to drive away.

She shoved the key in the ignition, lips burning from his kiss, and ground the gears as she pulled away, cursing him, herself, Likely Cove and even the Greater Regional District.

She glared at him through the rearview mirror as she drove away.

He was standing under a streetlight, smiling a big, goofy, happy grin. He raised an arm in salute, waving at her as she rounded the corner and roared away.

She felt like sticking her finger out the window in a very rude gesture.

# 5

THE REST OF THE WEEK she prayed for rain, but the weather didn't oblige.

When Annabelle opened her eyes Sunday morning, the sun was poking through the gauzy curtains on her bedroom window, and the sky was clear blue.

Her stomach filled with butterflies. She was going to have to keep her date with Ben, and somehow she was going to have to persuade him to do business with her.

Well, she had a whole day to do it in.

She dithered for an hour, getting more agitated and out of sorts with each passing moment, rushing in and out of the shower, shaving her legs, painting her toe-nails pink, trying to figure out what to wear and whether or not she ought to pack a lunch and why in hell she'd ever agreed to this in the first place.

*Business, Annabelle. Remember that it's business.*

Could it be she didn't want it to be business? The thought of Ben's kiss had interfered with her concentration the past few days.

At nine forty-five there was a forceful rap on her door.

"Morning, Annabelle." His maddening grin was intact, and the sheer size of him was intimidating. He wore faded, worn blue denims that fit his slim hips like a second skin, and a gray sweatshirt with the sleeves hacked off right at the top of his broad shoulders. His skin was deeply tanned, just as she remembered. The muscles of his upper arms, which she also remembered in vivid detail, were impressive and smoothly defined and sexy as hell.

She managed an imitation of a smile and stepped back to let him come in. What was it about him that made her feel so damned flustered...apart from the fact that he was so attractive it took her breath away?

"You ready? I hope you didn't eat any breakfast. You didn't, did you?" He cocked an eyebrow, and she shook her head.

He grinned again, that ingenuous, disarming grin that had become familiar enough to sneak into her dreams.

"Wonderful, because I'm starving." His intense gaze traveled down her white cotton T-shirt and sedate khaki walking shorts and he nodded approval. "You look great. Maybe you should grab a light jacket. It can get chilly even in hot weather on the bike. And a swimming suit. We'll want to swim by afternoon. Unless you'd rather skinny-dip. We could do that easy enough—there won't be anyone but us around."

The look she gave him made him laugh outright. "And don't forget your sunglasses. You'll need them on the motorcycle."

God, he was bossy. "We'll take my car. I've never ridden on a motorcycle in my life." The thought of it made her even more on edge.

"No problem. I'll drive and you just hang on. On a day like this, a bike's the only way to go."

She considered arguing and didn't bother. *Save it for the big issues, Annabelle. Before the day's over, there's bound to be something you'll need all your energy for. Like talking business to this crazy man.*

"But if you absolutely hate the bike after we ride downtown for breakfast," he was saying, "I promise we'll come back here and get your car, okay?"

So he was willing to compromise, now and then. When it suited him. She'd have to figure out how to use that to her own advantage.

"Agreed," she told him shortly.

He waited, whistling a cheerful tune while she went into her bedroom and found a blue Windbreaker, rejected a skimpy yellow bikini for her modest black tank suit, and raked through her hair with a wide-tooth comb before she balanced her sunglasses on top of her head. She stuffed everything else into her canvas handbag and went back into the living room.

"All ready?" He was standing with his hands shoved into the back pockets of his jeans, squinting at the framed Picasso print she had on the wall. "Man, I've always thought this guy had some weird slant on female anatomy, and this proves it," he remarked. "Three breasts, two sets of eyes, one leg. You'd almost think he had a shot or two of Rico's home brew when he painted this."

It had always been her favorite print. Well, plainly he knew beans all about art, she decided with a sniff.

"Shall we go?" There was a touch of frost in her tone. She led the way out, far too conscious of him close beside her.

Outside, she eyed the huge motorcycle with trepidation. Ben tugged on a well-worn black helmet and unsnapped a shiny new green one from the saddle. Before she could protest, he took her glasses off and gently fitted the helmet over her head.

She could feel her carefully fluffed hair collapsing like a deflated soufflé beneath the weight of the helmet.

He snapped the chin strap in place and gave her a long look before he nodded. "I figured green was right on you. Let's put your purse in here." He tucked it into a carrier on the back of the bike. "Now, put these on—" he handed her the glasses "—and climb on behind me."

Ben swung one long, jeans-clad leg over the saddle and balanced the machine upright, giving her an encouraging nod when she hesitated.

There was nothing to do but get on. Feeling clumsy, out of her element, and genuinely frightened, she climbed on behind him, wiping the perspiration on her palms onto the legs of her shorts.

Merciful heaven, there wasn't much room on this thing. She was tucked in right against his backside. She found handholds beneath her and clung to them, her heart racing, doing her best to keep at least a modest bit of distance between Ben's buttocks and her own wide-apart legs.

"Here, rest your feet on these pegs." He donned a pair of dark glasses himself and then pulled the bike away from the curb.

A scream rose in her throat as the machine tilted far too far over to one side. She abandoned the handholds and clenched both arms around Ben's waist. He accelerated, and in seconds it felt as if they were flying along the side streets. He reached down and patted her tightly clenched fists, locked around his midsection in a death grip.

"Relax, and lean the same way I do!" he hollered.

It was so…unprotected on this thing. She was aware of fresh air racing past, sunshine, exhaust, and the panicked hammering of her heart in her ears as she tried her best to follow his instructions.

He headed toward the downtown area, and in slow stages, Annabelle began to adjust to the sensations of acceleration and power, the terrifying tilt when they rounded corners, the easy way Ben's body related to the machine beneath them, and the competent, strong movements of his arms and torso as he drove. The bike might have been an extension of his body, so gracefully did he maneuver it.

By the time he nosed into a parking spot in front of a restaurant, turned the motor off and balanced the bike as she climbed shakily off, Annabelle thought that maybe she wasn't going to hate riding a motorcycle after all.

Well, she wouldn't mind riding behind Ben on his motorcycle, she revised. Her heart was pounding and adrenaline coursed through her veins. She felt alive, filled with giddy delight. Her earlier bad temper had disappeared, blown away with the breeze.

He pulled his helmet off and gently lifted hers away from her ruined hairdo.

"So what's the verdict, boss?" He was trying to sound flippant, but she could tell he was anxious about whether she'd enjoyed the ride.

She tried to salvage her hairdo by running her fingers through it and decided it was hopeless. "I guess we can take the bike." She didn't want to sound too enthusiastic.

"Hey, that's my girl." He wrapped a muscular arm around her shoulders and gave her an exuberant hug, keeping his arm in place as he led the way down the street and into a narrow café.

Ben waved a cheerful hand at the cadaverous young man behind the counter in the small diner. "Morning, Henry, how's it going? Can you make us two of your breakfast specials?" He led her to a booth by the window, and within moments mugs of steaming coffee and glasses of chilled orange juice were in front of them on the oilcloth-covered table.

"Good to see you, Ben." Henry had a red bandanna tied around his forehead and a rose tattoo on the back of one hand. He smiled and shook Annabelle's hand when Ben introduced them. "Food'll be up in just a couple minutes."

Conscious of her hips, Annabelle considered toast, marmalade and coffee a lavish extravagance in the morning.

Obviously, Henry and Ben had a different idea of breakfast.

Two bowls of fresh fruit salad were followed by a platter of buckwheat pancakes with golden fried potatoes on the side. A generous bowl of baked beans was accompanied by scrambled eggs, a tall stack of toast made from what tasted like homemade bread, puffy hot biscuits, jam, and an assortment of muffins in a wicker basket.

At first, Annabelle tried only to nibble, but one bite led to another and soon she was munching down generous portions of almost everything. "I can't believe I'm eating all this," she groaned, taking a bite of feather-light biscuit lathered with black currant jam. "The food is fantastic. How did you ever find this place, Ben?"

"Actually, Henry found *me*," Ben explained. "He's a vegetarian cook. He uses only fresh ingredients, and he needed free-range eggs. My chickens keep hatching new batches of chicks that then lay dozens of eggs, far more than I can ever use—and I'm not interested in selling the damn things. So Henry and I run on the barter system—he comes out and gets eggs and I get breakfast whenever I'm in town. It's a good deal for us both." He took another huge helping of potato and then slathered jam on a thick slab of toast, breaking off a chunk and feeding it to Annabelle. His fingers stroked across her cheek, and she told herself it was probably accidental.

"Eat up. You'll need lots of energy today," he warned, blue eyes twinkling. "Riding a bike is tough exercise."

"If I eat much more, I won't fit on the seat," she moaned.

"You could eat a dozen breakfasts like this and still fit nicely on that seat," he assured her. His tone was light, but there was a flicker of heat in his blue eyes that sent shivers down her spine.

The shivers were still there half an hour later, but they had nothing to do with Ben's eyes. Instead, they centered on his motorcycle.

She clung breathlessly to his lean waist as they flew along the narrow, winding road that led to Likely Cove. She'd driven this route out to the cove dozens of times, but she'd never really noticed it the way she did now.

The road was carved into the side of the mountain, and a flimsy barrier was all that separated the highway from a sheer cliff that dropped hundreds of yards down to the mirror-clear surface of Okanagan Lake. Tortuous twists and turns made her catch her breath as Ben confidently swooped and swung the motorcycle up and down hills and around curves. It was a little like flying in a very small, open plane, and she should have been scared but instead she was exhilarated, loving the feeling of soaring through the open air.

They communicated with gestures more than words; conversation was difficult because of their helmets and the wind. All the same, there was an intense intimacy, being as close as she was to Ben's body.

She could feel the powerful muscles working in his arms and torso as he maneuvered the heavy machine, and she was again intimately aware that her crotch was pressed tight against his bottom.

She was also aware of the heat of his body. It penetrated not only his clothing, but hers as well, a seductive, pervasive human warmth that reminded her of how it had felt to be in his arms. She fought those fantasies at first, but as the miles passed, she abandoned all her reservations and allowed herself to dream in vivid detail how it would feel to be loved by him.

Annabelle had lost all sense of time and place when Ben at last steered the bike off the highway and down the rutted gravel road she remembered so well—the road that led to Likely Cove.

He braked beside the ramshackle shed she'd noticed on her trips out here. It was built only a few feet from the water's edge. Ben balanced the bike upright until Annabelle climbed off, and then he lowered it onto the kickstand.

She was surprised to find that her legs were trembling. She fumbled with her helmet, feeling disoriented and light-headed. The sun glittered off the wide, empty expanse of dark green lake water. Higher up the hill, the acres of land that belonged to Pinetree Developments sat baking in the sun.

Well, they actually belonged more to the bank than to her company, she revised.

She wondered if this was the right time to mention the offer again, but couldn't bring herself to do it. The bike ride had lulled her into a delicious lethargy. She didn't want to spoil it by talking business.

Besides, she had all day. The exact moment would arrive, and she'd take advantage of it, she assured herself.

God, it was hot. And quiet, as well. Deserted. She'd somehow overlooked how alone they'd be here at the cove. Birds chirped in the nearby pines and a small plane flew overhead, but there wasn't another person anywhere around; probably for miles, Annabelle concluded.

"Peaceful, isn't it?" Ben unlocked the padlock on the doors at the front of the shed and effortlessly slid the small aluminum motorboat it housed down the incline and into the lake. He returned to the bike and began transferring plastic grocery bags and a small cooler from the saddlebags into the boat, retrieving her handbag last and giving it to her just before he took her hand in a courtly gesture and helped her aboard.

With a strong shove from his booted foot, the vessel floated into deeper water and in one smooth, strong motion he leaped in, and a moment later had the motor running.

A kind of panic came over Annabelle as the shore receded and they headed toward the small, treed island in the middle of the wide expanse of water.

What in heaven's name was she doing? If this excursion turned out badly, she certainly couldn't call a cab or hitch a ride home. She'd put herself in a position of total dependency on a man she'd known for exactly one week.

What was wrong with her head?

Ben's long legs collided with hers just then, and he turned from guiding the boat to smile at her—a lazy, happy, contented smile.

"Thanks for coming with me today, Annabelle." The wind blew his thick brown hair over his wide forehead, and he tipped the dark glasses up so she could see his eyes, bluer than the lake or the sky, with an expression in them that underlined his words, a sort of humorous tenderness that reassured her.

"I love this island. I love coming over here. And having you along today makes everything perfect."

Her uncertainty of a moment ago fled, and she found herself relaxing. After all, Ben used to be an RCMP officer. Surely she could trust a former RCMP officer to act like a gentleman and bring her back safely at the end of the day.

The boat grated on sand, and Ben lifted the motor and used an oar to guide them closer to shore. He stepped out into calf-deep water and hauled the boat up, then took Annabelle's hand and helped her out.

"Welcome to Paradise." He didn't relinquish her hand. Instead, he led her along a faint path that meandered into the pines. "There's a place over this way where there's a sort of beach, and that sun is getting hotter by the minute. What d'ya say to a swim?"

She was sweating, and the water looked more inviting by the moment. "I'll change over there in the trees. There're no snakes on this island, are there, Ben?"

"None that I've ever seen. But holler if a bear comes nosing around. I'll be right there to save you."

She gave him a scathing look. "I greatly doubt there're any bears out here, either."

"Just my lousy luck," he deadpanned, unbuttoning his jeans and stripping them off, revealing brief blue nylon trunks. They weren't bikinis, quite. But they weren't exactly boxer trunks, either.

She watched, mesmerized, as he tugged the gray shirt up over his head and discarded it along with his jeans. She stared at the muscles across his chest, a chest coated with swirls of dark hair that led like a marching band down to his stomach, and her eyes dropped against her will to the scrap of blue nylon at his hips. Just like the cutoffs he'd worn that first day they met, this garment didn't hide an awful lot of him. Heat swelled inside her.

And then he caught her looking. Mortified, she swung around and crashed into the bushes, stumbling along until she felt protected enough to strip off her own clothes and struggle into the tank suit. Her fingers trembled, and confusion filled her.

There was just no denying the fact that he excited her sexually. It had been a long time since she'd been physically attracted to a man this way. Fifteen years, to be exact. She'd been a girl, young and romantic, in Greece for a holiday, and she'd married Theodore Winslow because he'd stirred these very same intense feelings inside her.

Feelings of lust, she told herself, wishing desperately there was some way to turn them off at will.

She'd been a young girl when she met Theodore, and it was easy for a girl to mistake lust for love—especially a girl as unsophisticated and naive as she had been.

It was the single biggest mistake she'd ever made, marrying Theodore instead of just sleeping with him. At least the bitter memories had kept her safe all these years from making the same mistake again.

She'd had lovers, certainly. Temporary, ultimately forgettable affairs—disappointing affairs—that never came close to piercing the protective wrapping she'd built up around her heart and her emotions.

*So you find this Ben attractive. So what? You're not
a naive twenty-year-old anymore, Annabelle. You can
control whatever happens between you. And you're
certainly not going to marry him, so what are you
afraid of?*

What, indeed? She snapped the black elastic straps
securely onto her shoulders and tugged the back of her
suit down. Then she modestly tucked her lacy underwear into her handbag, gathered up her shorts and shirt
and walked back to where Ben waited on the rocky
shoreline.

His eyes were appreciative without being bold as he
looked her up and down. "You must swim a lot. That's
a real swimmer's bathing suit. I noticed there's a pool
at your building." He gestured at the towel he'd spread
carefully beside his own on the large, flat rock. "Sit
down."

She did, stretching her legs out and doing her best to
hold her tummy in, groping in her handbag for the sun-
block lotion. "I try to swim every day. It's the only regular exercise I get."

"It shows. You look great, toned and lean in all the
right places." She had to smile at him. It was exactly the
right thing to say. Ben had a knack for saying things that
made her feel good.

"Here, you'd better let me rub some of that stuff on
your back before you burn." He moved to kneel behind her, reaching for the bottle of sun block she'd just
smoothed on her arms and legs. He poured some of the
warm liquid out onto the palm of his hand, and began
to smooth it over her shoulders and down the skin
bared by the modest swimsuit. "This is all going to
come off the minute you get in the water, you know."

"No, it won't." She slid her sunglasses on, hiding her eyes, afraid they'd reveal the pure animal pleasure it gave her to have him touch her like this with his strong, callused hands. "It's a new kind. It's supposed to be waterproof."

"So besides swimming in your spare time, what else do you do?"

He was rubbing the lotion in as if it was skin softener, in big, firm circles, and little up-and-down strokes, his hands pleasantly rough against her skin. Bewitched by the hypnotic delight of his touch, she didn't even monitor the starkly honest answer she gave to his question.

"I don't have any spare time. I bought a mountain bike six months ago, and I've used it exactly once. I have a stack of murder mysteries I haven't had time to read, and a lifetime membership at a gym that I got talked into joining last year. I've used the facilities three times in eleven months."

He stroked her shoulders, beginning at her neck and letting his hands move in rhythmic motions down to her elbows and then back up again. Something in her lower regions was melting like butter.

"What you're telling me," he went on in that low, captivating voice, "is that you don't take any time for yourself. Maybe you need to hire more people, Annabelle. It sounds like you need a chance to relax."

"Can't afford it," she murmured, eyes closed behind the dark lenses, senses lulled by his hands. "Market's gone soft."

"It'll come back up again, especially in this valley." His hands were still now, resting on her shoulders. "You know, your skin feels so good, I hate to stop touching it." His voice wasn't quite steady.

Annabelle opened her eyes. She was leaning back, almost leaning on him. She realized that he was waiting for her to make the next move, allowing her to decide whether to move the few inches that separated them or . . . Good Lord, what was she doing?

"It's time for a swim. Coming?" Her own voice was none too steady, either. She got up quickly, without looking at him, and walked down to the water. She waded in up to her knees and then dove forward and began to swim, gasping at first at the shocking contrast between hot sun and cold water. Then, as her body adjusted, she welcomed the cool sanctuary of the lake.

A splash behind her signaled Ben's shallow dive. A moment later, he surfaced beside her. "Aagh, this water's cold," he gasped, and she laughed at the horrified expression on his face. "Want to do laps? It'll keep us from freezing."

"From here to where?" She was treading water. "I'm not up for swimming to the mainland."

"See that big tree hanging down? Let's go to there and back."

They swam out a distance and then stroked along lazily, parallel with the shore. Ben was a strong, easy swimmer, and Annabelle felt a little proud of her own effortless crawl.

When they reached the tree, they turned in unison.

"Race you back." Ben suddenly began an energetic stroke that soon had him yards ahead of Annabelle.

"Cheat!" she called after him, putting all her effort into the race. He won, of course, but she was within a few feet of him by the time they drew close to where the towels lay on the rock.

"That was totally unfair, Ben Baxter," she accused in an outraged tone, panting a little as she rolled onto her back and recovered. "You didn't give me a fighting chance. You took unfair advantage. And I'm a woman, and you're supposed to be a gentleman."

Ben laughed and dove under the water, and she shrieked as a hand closed over her ankle. She lashed out with her other foot, but it, too, was captured in a strong grip, and with just enough time to fill her lungs, she was dragged underwater.

He released her ankles and playfully grabbed her waist instead, and as she struggled, their bodies intertwined, cool, slithery skins touching, arms and legs and torsos juxtaposed.

Annabelle stopped fighting him and put her hands on his shoulders.

For a timeless instant, they held on to one another, motionless, bodies tinted faintly green and gold by the sun that penetrated the water. Then, breathless, they shot to the surface like corks, emerging gasping and laughing, with soaked hair dripping into their eyes.

"You're an absolute menace, Ben Baxter. You almost drowned me." Annabelle swam to shallow water and stood, pushing the wet strands of hair out of her eyes, smoothing it back on her skull, laughing at him. "I'll bet I have bruises on my ankles." She pretended to limp to shore and collected one of the towels, rubbing herself dry.

He was right behind her. "I didn't really grab you hard enough to hurt you, did I?" He was concerned, and she had to laugh and shake her head.

"I'm not that fragile."

"Want me to dry your back?"

"I don't trust you anymore, pulling me under like that." The truth was, she didn't trust herself with him touching her.

"I just wanted to see if you were really a mermaid, is all." Water still dripped down his craggy face, catching in his mustache and glistening in the thick mat of hair on his broad chest. "Besides, I had to work like hell to stay ahead of you out there. You're younger than I am. I deserved a head start."

She laughed up at him, taunting him, flirting and loving it. "I'm also a better swimmer."

He squinted at her, blue eyes filled with laughter. "Prettier, too," he drawled.

She wasn't going to comment on that. The wet blue nylon at his hips outlined his body in breathtaking detail, and his thighs were sleek and strong. She thought of being in his arms underwater, and she shivered.

He moved to the shady spot under a tree where he'd put the cooler, and, opening it, rummaged around inside. "Swimming always makes me thirsty. You want lunch now, or just something to drink? We've got my homemade wine, a couple bottles of beer, bottled water, a can of lemonade."

"You brought all that along?"

"I wanted to impress you." His tone was teasing, but she recognized the note of truth in what he said and a giddy delight filled her. It was heady stuff, having a gorgeous man like this trying to impress her.

"I'd like a glass of that homemade wine you keep bragging about, please."

"Coming right up." He unearthed plastic glasses and uncorked a dark green bottle, carefully pouring some and handing it to her with a mock bow.

The sun had almost dried her suit. She settled on the towel and sipped the cool, tart wine, letting it roll around on her tongue and slip little by little down her throat.

"Ambrosia," she declared, only half joking. She was no expert, but it tasted wonderful. An unusual feeling came creeping over her as he poured a glass for himself and sat down beside her.

It was a feeling of lightness that seemed to pervade every cell of her being, as if the wine were bubbling inside her arteries and veins, making her feel impossibly young and carefree.

"What do you call this?" She searched through her limited vocabulary of generic wines. "Chardonnay? Pinot Noire? Riesling?"

"Summer wine. I just call it summer wine."

The stillness of a hot afternoon had settled over the island and the lake—a somnolent peace that made the city and all the problems it represented seem ridiculously unimportant and faraway.

At last, Annabelle identified what she was feeling. She was happy—plain old happy—and it felt peculiar.

She hadn't felt this entirely happy in a long time. In fact, she couldn't remember exactly when and where she'd felt this way before.

She lifted her glass in a toast. "To summer wine. And to Paradise, without the serpent."

But if a serpent represented temptation and pure outright lust, Annabelle mused, there was no doubt it was alive and well and living right here on Paradise Island.

# 6

"HOW ABOUT IF I TAKE you on a guided tour of Paradise as soon as we rest a little and dry off?" Ben was lounging beside her, and she felt too comfortable and happy even to rub more suntan lotion on her arms and legs. What the heck, the stuff was supposed to be waterproof.

"Will you give me a running commentary on all the tourist traps and show me the tree where the forbidden fruit grows?" She turned her head to look at him, and loved the way his eyes twinkled at her nonsense.

"Absolutely. It'll take time, though. This place is huge."

"We'd better rest up before we leave, then." She settled back on her towel, closing her eyes and wriggling into a hollow on the rocks.

Without warning, he reached over with a free hand and gripped the back of her neck, bringing her lips to his in one unexpected, hard, smacking kiss. He tasted of wine and sunshine.

She giggled when he let her go and he gave her a scathing look.

"So now my passionate kisses are funny?"

"Your mustache tickles my nose."

"Then we'll just have to practice until you get used to it, won't we?" There was a banked warmth in his eyes and his voice, and he took her free hand in his and held it, stroking the back with his fingers, then raising it to his lips and kissing, nipping, licking each finger, turning her hand over and using his teeth on her palm in a way that brought a rush of heat into her midsection.

She tried to ignore the tingling in her breasts, the warmth between her legs. A tiny, ruthless voice in her head nagged, *Take advantage of the moment, Annabelle. Bring up the offer on the cove right now. He promised he'd talk about it rationally if you came out here with him. Do it now, when you're at ease with one another. Do it while he's off-balance.*

Except that he wasn't the only one off-balance here. She was aroused, and she knew he was, as well. His swimming suit neatly outlined his obvious erection, and the intriguing bulge did nothing to dampen her own feelings.

But the merciless voice of reason persisted. *Talk to him, Annabelle.*

"Ben," she began, appalled at the tremor in her voice. "Ben, you said we'd discuss the offer on the cove today. Have you given it any more thought?"

"I haven't changed my mind." His tone was casual. "I really can't imagine any offer or any situation that would make me change my mind." He went on holding her hand, tracing lines in her palm with one rough forefinger.

She cleared her throat. "We're prepared to make every concession." Part of this she'd thought over in the past few days, part she was making up on the spur of the moment. "For instance, we'd expand the offer to assure you unlimited access to the cove, of course. We'd make sure your boathouse stays exactly where it is. And you mentioned being unhappy with the way development was being handled in the Okanagan. Perhaps I could negotiate a deal where you had some input on the way the land above the cove is developed—lot size, trees left standing, that sort of thing."

He was looking at her now and frowning. "Tell me something. Exactly why is this deal so important to you? When you talk about it, you get all tense. Your voice changes, you stiffen up." He held one of her hands aloft, and she realized she'd unwittingly clenched her fist.

She uncurled it, embarrassed at being so transparent.

His voice sharpened, and his blue gaze seemed to impale her. She was reminded that he was probably an old hand at interrogation.

"Who exactly owns the land surrounding the cove, anyhow, Annabelle?"

"Pinetree Developments, at the moment. But overseas interests have made a bid for the parcel." It was true, as far as it went.

She wasn't about to bare her soul, confess how desperate her company's need was for the sale. "And who owns Pinetree Developments?" He sounded only mildly curious.

For the space of a heartbeat, she didn't answer. "Actually, Johnny Calvados, Cyril Lisk. And me. Pinetree is a subsidiary of Midas."

"I see." He nodded, as if she was only confirming what he already suspected. "And the sale to the investors hinges on you getting me to sell you the cove, is that right?" It was a statement more than a question.

"More or less." All more, no less.

"And you stand to make a good profit on this whole thing." Again, it wasn't a question.

For a moment, she longed to spill out the whole story, throw herself at his mercy, beg him to save her company.

She knew he was sexually attracted to her. More than that, she also sensed that he liked her—liked the person she was when she wasn't being a real-estate wheeler-dealer.

And she couldn't ask him to do it, because of those very things.

"We stand to make a profit, yes, but not at your expense, Ben. I want to buy the cove from you for every cent that you believe it's worth, so that you benefit. It's a business deal. It could be lucrative for both of us." She kept her voice steady and light. "After all, I have every right to want to make a profit, to . . . to be a success at what I do."

He nodded, squinting out over the lake, still frowning. "I've got no argument with that, and I wish I could do this for you." He turned and looked into her eyes. "The trouble is, I just can't. The cove isn't just a piece of land to me. It represents principles, feelings I have about what's right and wrong. Can you understand that, Annabelle?"

A week ago, she wouldn't have understood at all. Today, being here with him, she did. She nodded, knowing there would be little point in bringing the matter up again. "I understand. If that's how you feel, then we'll leave it like that."

She'd lost the battle, and right now, she wouldn't think about what the ramifications of that loss would be. The day was too sunny, the atmosphere too peaceful, the lake too calming. She'd worry about it tomorrow. It was almost a relief to have it over with.

"Thanks." He got to his feet in one easy, fluid movement and pulled her up beside him. "Now, I think it's time for that guided tour I promised you."

For the next hour, they strolled around the tiny island, talking and laughing. He showed her where a family of raccoons lived, where the bluebirds nested, and where he'd seen a doe and her fawn early one morning.

"It couldn't have been a deer, Ben. How would deer have gotten over here in the first place?"

"Probably swum. Or maybe they've just always been here, one generation after the other."

"But the place would be overrun by now, wouldn't it? I don't think deer practice birth control."

"Maybe these do. They're highly unique animals. After all, they live in Paradise. Here, anything's possible."

"Lucky things," she said wistfully.

They ambled back to where the boat was and had lunch late in the afternoon, when the sun was already setting toward the mountains.

Annabelle was starving, despite the enormous breakfast she'd consumed. Over the man-size sandwiches Ben had packed, they talked about books they'd read, argued over movies they'd seen, exchanged easy recipes they'd discovered that produced a reasonable dinner in fifteen minutes or less, and discussed which fast-food places they preferred. Ben told her about growing up an only child in a small prairie town, always feeling responsible for his mother.

"Dad died when I was ten. Mom was sort of fragile. She'd never really dealt with any of the realities of life because Dad had always taken care of her. He sort of passed the responsibility on to me. I was working after school and taking care of the family finances by the time I was fourteen. Looking back, I must have been about the most boring teenager in western Canada."

She doubted that. With his looks, he'd probably had half the girls in town in love with him.

"Is your mother still alive?"

Ben shook his head. "She died two years after I joined the RCMP. Even though I felt responsible for her, I was never really close to my mother. She lived in a sort of dreamworld, and as I got older I resented her dependency on me. I felt I'd missed out on being young, I guess."

Annabelle thought about his life-style now, and she understood a little better his reasons for choosing a carefree existence at this point in his life. "You must have been very lonely," she said softly, thinking of that serious young boy forced to grow up too quickly.

"Sometimes, but I was lucky," he said with a wide grin. "My grandfather had a little house not far from us, and I could always go and talk to him when things got me down. He was a huge old Norwegian. He'd been a sailor and he had endless stories to tell, most of them off-color. He taught me to swear and play poker, and how to make wine. He made the best wine I've ever tasted."

"Better than yours?" She gave him a teasing glance, expecting him to deny it, but he surprised her.

"Much better than mine. Granddad had the Bacchus touch."

She'd bet there was a great deal of that Norwegian grandfather in Ben. "Did he happen to have blue eyes?"

He grinned at her, and winked. "Now, how did you guess?"

They ate in companionable silence for a time, and then Ben said, "Now tell me about your childhood, Annabelle. Tell me what kind of little girl you were." He produced two fat red apples and a bag of oatmeal cookies from his cooler. He handed her one of each, biting into his apple with a satisfying crunch and using the cookie as a chaser.

She shot him a curious look. "You know, I don't think I've ever had a man ask me that before. None of them ever seemed curious about my childhood."

He lifted an eyebrow and swallowed. "Like I said once before, the other men you know don't exactly sound like prime specimens to me."

"And you figure you are? A prime specimen?"

He didn't rise to the challenge the way she thought he would. He reached over and tousled her hair instead. "Don't change the subject, Annabelle. You're good at deflecting questions about yourself, but I'm not going to let you off the hook this time. I'm going to hold you captive here until you tell me how it was for you, growing up. What were your parents like?"

She rubbed the apple with a paper napkin until it shone. "I was an only child, just like you," she began, turning the apple over in her hands and staring at it as if it held her memories. "My parents were wealthy, and well into middle age when they had me. I was a bit of a shock to them, accustomed as they were to a life-style that didn't include children. We had a huge house just outside London. Daddy was a barrister and worked in the City. Mummy was involved in various charity organizations. She was hardly ever home."

"Are they both still alive?"

"My mother died two years ago. My father's in his seventies now, rattling round in the same house I was born in, although he's not as well-off as he was. He's had to sell off most of the land, and he only has a housekeeper to help keep it up. He really ought to sell. I've tried to talk him into coming to Canada, but he won't hear of it. Unfortunately, we're not close, my father and I. He feels I'm a great disappointment to him."

She looked up and met his intense blue eyes. "Why's that?"

She was on shaky ground here. She shrugged off the question. "Oh, I think he wanted me to be like Mother—marry well and fritter away my days hosting teas and playing bridge. And of course he doesn't approve of Canada at all. To him it's still one of the outposts of the Empire."

"Were you close to your parents when you were little?"

She drew in a deep breath, relieved that he didn't probe for the real reasons her father had all but disowned her. "Close to them?" She shook her head. "Not at all. I was a brat, a spoiled child; I had a nanny, far too many toys, my own pony, beautiful clothes, but I didn't really see much of my mother and father. I saw even less of them when I was sent off to school at seven."

"Boarding school?" He took her hand again, stroking her fingers one by one in an absent sort of way.

She nodded. "English children from wealthy families are always sent off to boarding school. I attended the one my mother had gone to—a great, cold mausoleum called Barkely House. I was dreadfully homesick at first, I had no idea how to get along with other children. I really was an impossible child."

"Poor little girl." There was no irony in his tone, only compassion, and to her amazement, it brought the sting of tears to her eyes. She blinked hard, astonished that long-ago memories should affect her this deeply after all this time.

"Ridiculous, for a child to be such a social ostrich, isn't it? I finally made friends with another girl, who was as much a misfit as I was, and things got better."

"What was her name?"

"Beatrice. What drew us together was our hair. We were both redheads. Hers was a flaming mop of curls, and of course with that unfortunate name, everyone called her Beets." Annabelle smiled and shook her head. "I haven't thought about her in years. She married an impoverished earl and moved to Spain. Last I heard, she had seven kids and was running a bed-and-breakfast."

"And you got married, moved to Canada and became a real-estate hotshot."

She gave him a sidelong glance. "Something like that." She didn't feel at all like a hotshot—not at all. Not here, not now.

"What would you be if you weren't in real estate?" He'd laced his fingers with hers and rested their clasped hands on his thigh. She was conscious of the soft hairs on his leg, of the firm muscle and warm skin under her hand. She wanted to stroke her fingers over that skin, but she resisted.

What *would* she be? Annabelle hadn't thought about anything except real estate for so long that she needed some time to answer.

Ben waited silently while she thought about it.

"I'd be a preschool teacher," she finally said in a soft, dreamy voice. "I think working all day with really young kids would be a great way to spend my time."

"So why don't you give it a shot?"

She turned to stare at him. "We can't all rush off chasing our dreams, Ben." Her tone was sarcastic. "I have responsibilities. I have to earn a living. Other people depend on me. I'm not in business on my own, you know. I have two partners to consider." She felt irrationally angry with him, because again she knew she wasn't telling him the real reason at all.

He shrugged. "They're big people. They'd survive if you decided to do something else with your life." The certainty in his voice made her momentarily furious.

What did he know about any of it? Her reasons for staying in real estate were complex, all mixed up with old, deep pain and anger; reasons she didn't have any intention of remembering right now. Why did he have to probe and pick at things better left alone?

Especially right now, when she was enjoying herself. She was having a sort of time-out day, and she didn't want to spoil it. She didn't want *him* to spoil it. She wanted to stretch the hours left like elastic, till the last possible moment. Until she had to get in his boat and go back and face her real life again, she wanted to pretend this was all there was. She wanted, just for today, to *feel* instead of think.

He sensed her anger. "Sorry, Annabelle. I guess I remember too clearly what it's like to work at something you'd rather not do. I'm like one of those reformed smokers who thinks everybody should quit just because I did." He got to his feet. "Hey, you want to try fishing? It's a great way of getting rid of frustration."

"Fishing?" She'd never been fishing in her entire life. She didn't even like to eat fish, unless it was a can of tuna.

"It's a nice way to spend an afternoon," he assured her.

Grudgingly at first and then with growing enthusi-
asm, she let him show her how to hold the rod, how to
cast, how to reel in. It was nice, because he stood behind her, his arms encircling her, showing her the finer
points of casting.

She messed the line up again and again, but he was
the most patient of teachers. Several times, they
laughed so hard at her inept efforts, they could barely
stand.

After a while, she started to get the hang of it, but it
took every ounce of concentration to keep the rod, the
reel, the fishing line all in order; and with him standing
close, it was doubly hard.

The sun slipped behind the mountain when she
wasn't looking, and the heat hung over the lake in a
curtain of bluish haze. Ben put the rods away; neither
of them had caught a thing, for which Annabelle was
grateful. She really didn't want to hook anything alive.

"How about I make a fire? I brought some wieners.
We could roast them for supper."

Together they gathered twigs, bantering back and
forth mostly about nothing, and Ben built a perfect little fire. He shaved willow branches into pointed hold-
ers for the wieners, and they browned them over the
flames as twilight deepened. They ate them along with
bags of potato crisps, as they sat on their towels in the
grass, drinking the last of the wine.

Annabelle got up and went down to the lake when
she was done and scooped some water up to wash her
mouth and hands, and when she turned, he was standing by the fire, watching her with an intensity that sent
shock waves through her.

"Come here, Annabelle." His voice was husky.

She went toward him slowly, feeling hypnotized by the intensity of his blue gaze, by the electricity that danced between them like fox fire. When she was near enough, he drew her, step by step, into his arms, curling one strong hand at the back of her neck, gently pulling her close so their bodies touched.

"I've been waiting to hold you like this, all day." He smoothed her hair back and touched her nose with his own. "I've been trying my damnedest not to scare you, not to rush you. I've been trying to be polite, and now the whole day's almost gone and we haven't practiced this kissing thing at all."

His lips descended, gently at first, to claim hers.

This time she had no desire to giggle. She shivered instead, and he wrapped his arms close around her, molding his body to hers so that her breasts touched his chest.

"You taste good. You feel good." His tongue slid along the seam of her lips until she opened for him, and he explored her mouth, tilting his head one way and then the other to find a perfect fit.

His fingers cradled her head again, one hand slipping down to touch her neck and stroke it. Tentatively her tongue met his. Then liquid fire came to life in her belly and at that instant, his kiss became greedy.

He'd pulled his jeans on over his swim trunks but left his torso bare. She lifted her arms and wrapped them around him, thrilling to the heat of his skin, the hard, hair-roughened texture of him. She could feel his heart hammering against his ribs, and she understood that he was holding back, going slow, deliberately inviting her to set the pace.

She ran her hands down his back, trembling when her touch made him quiver.

"Annabelle . . . God, Bella . . ." His tone was urgent, his words muffled by the hungry joining of their lips. "You're beautiful." She slid her hands over his back again, touching his bare skin, reveling in the feel of him, the way his shoulders tapered sharply down to his narrow waist and hips. He quivered wherever she touched.

She gave herself permission to enjoy the moment, permission to react to his kisses.

*It's only kisses, after all. I won't think. I'll only feel.*

And it felt natural and right, so very right, to be in his arms this way. Her breasts pressed against his chest, and she could feel his erection, straining against the fabric of his jeans, hard and tempting against her abdomen. She moved, a rhythmic swaying motion of her hips that she was helpless to control, and he groaned.

Her legs felt weak, as if she couldn't stand without his support.

His hand came down and cupped her breast, rubbing the fabric of her shirt in tantalizing, slow circles, back and forth over the nipple in a maddening dance, and helplessly she reacted, lifting to his touch, pulsing against him.

She was hungry, so hungry for him. She had been since the night on the beach, when he'd first kissed her.

His hands moved down her, learning her intimate parts, cupping her buttocks and pulling her up and into the hard curve of his body.

"Bella?" There was a question in his strangled voice, and she was on fire, answering frantically, with her lips and her hands and her movements.

His hips rotated against hers, teasing, and the liquid heat that centered in her belly became unbearable, making her gasp and cry out.

"Let's get this off. I need to touch your skin. . . ." He tugged at her T-shirt, pulling it out of her shorts, starting gently and then in one rough, determined movement, drawing it up and over her head. He tossed it on the grass, and it took him only a moment to figure out the front hook on her lacy bra, and then with trembling fingers he slid the straps down and off her arms.

"Look at you! God, you're so lovely, so full and voluptuous." His hands cupped her heavy naked breasts, his thumbs teasing the already turgid nipples, sending electric currents of heat bolting down into her belly. When he released her for an instant to unfasten the snap at the waist of his jeans, she could hardly stand it.

He slid them over his hips, taking the blue swimming suit with them, and as he straightened, he drew her nipple into his mouth, tugging at it, rubbing his tongue over the tip, drawing it deep into his mouth in a regular, pulsing cadence.

Annabelle thought her heart would hammer its way out of her chest. When at last he released her breast, she drew back a little and looked at him. Naked, he was beautiful—the way a lithe and powerful animal was beautiful. His body was dusted with thick dark hair, his sex fully aroused and magnificent.

She reached out, hypnotized, and took him in her hand, hot and heavy and throbbing, and a sense of power mingled with the desire that pounded inside her when he closed his eyes and gasped from the pleasure of her touch.

He reached between them and deftly unfastened the button at the waistline of her shorts. He slid the zipper down, and shimmied shorts and panties over her hips, past her knees, his hot, wet mouth tracing a path of seduction from breasts to belly and back again.

Then he held her fast, steadying her as she stepped clumsily out of her clothing. His fingers explored the damp, moist, needy place between her legs. She rubbed against him, and he knew exactly where to touch, how to inflame. Her breathing came in short, desperate rasps, and her heart thundered as his knowing fingers stroked and circled.

With an impatient growl, he lifted her naked body, fitting it intimately to his, his arms corded and strong as steel against her back, cupping her buttocks, grinding her against him.

She wrapped her arms around his neck. Beyond thought, she lifted her legs until they encircled his waist, frantic to feel the long, hard shaft of him against her, inside her.

"Wait. Here, let's go over here... Soon, Bella, soon..." He carried her to where the towels were spread and lowered her onto them. She was only vaguely aware of the hard ground beneath her, the darkening sky above. The world was blotted out by his body and her desperate need.

Her arms were still linked around his neck, and she pulled him down to her, only half aware that she was murmuring against his lips in a frenzy of wanting, "Now, Ben. Please, now. Please ..."

In one long, fluid movement, he entered her, and a cry of exquisite pleasure spilled from her lips. He moved again, more insistently now, and she passed some marker that signaled the last of her control.

With a will of its own, her body rose to meet his, urging him on faster, harder, with a violence she'd never dreamed she possessed, until at last, she no longer knew which of them surged or which drew back.

Her climax came with soul-shattering intensity an instant before his, and as he shuddered and convulsed she held his body tightly against her, sucking in lungfuls of air as spasms of delight rocketed through her. Then his body seemed to crumble, nearly crushing her momentarily with his weight. She didn't mind. She was floating on waves of contentment.

He rolled to one side, cradling her in his arms, a faint sheen of sweat standing out on his forehead, arms trembling in the aftermath of passion. His blue eyes were heavy-lidded, searching her face anxiously. He seemed to relax when she smiled at him.

"So much for control," he whispered, nipping at her lips with gentle kisses. "And I didn't protect you, either. I planned to, while my brain was still working, but things got away on me."

His hand stroked her hair out of her eyes and then slid down her damp back, moving her into a more comfortable position against him. "You made me feel like a randy teenager, Bella. God knows, I sure acted like one."

"I wasn't exactly fighting you off." Her voice was languid. She felt too weak to move. She wanted him to go on holding her this way forever. She felt whole, in a way she couldn't ever remember feeling before, and she couldn't even bring herself to be embarrassed over the wanton way she'd begged him to love her.

"I'm not usually this irresponsible, Bella. I want you to know I don't have any nasty diseases." Her head was pillowed on his chest, and his voice rumbled pleasantly in her ear. She tried to remember exactly when he'd started calling her Bella.

No one else ever had, and she liked it.

"Me either. Any diseases." Sexually transmitted disease wasn't exactly something she'd had to consider in recent years.

"Is there a chance we'll be pregnant?"

His choice of words made her smile. She moved her head from side to side, feeling the texture of his chest hair on her skin.

"Not a chance."

He was silent for a long time. Then he sighed and said, "Too bad."

She lifted her head and looked into his face, to see if he was joking with her. "I thought we agreed that babies needed two parents."

His eyes held hers for a long heartbeat. "She'd have two parents. If that's what you wanted."

This was getting too complicated for her. Things were moving far too fast, in a direction she wasn't at all sure she wanted to travel.

Annabelle moved away from him and sat up, needing distance, needing to separate herself from the frightening closeness she felt.

"It's getting awfully dark. I can hardly see across the lake. Will we have trouble getting back in the dark?"

He sat up, too. "I've got a trouble light on the boat. You may have to hold it for me."

"We really ought to get started, then. I didn't realize how late it was getting." Niggling doubts were beginning to invade the languorous peace she'd felt. All day, she'd pretended that here and now was all there was; that real life had been suspended while they were on this tiny, perfect island.

She got up, self-conscious now of her nakedness.

He refused to let her leave him that way, however. He caught her by the shoulders and held her at arm's length, his eyes deliberately tracing down every inch of her body before he took her chin in his hand and tipped it up, forcing her to meet his eyes.

"Do you have any idea how lovely you are, my Bella? You're like a fantasy come true for me. I've thought of little else but you all week."

The same had been true for her, but she wouldn't admit it. Not now. She felt suddenly as if she'd revealed far more than her body to him, as if he'd penetrated parts of her soul. It terrified her.

He sensed her reticence, and with a sigh he dropped his hands and turned, searching for the clothing scattered here and there in the grass.

He found her panties, bra, shorts and shirt, smoothing them with clumsy, masculine care before he handed them to her, steadying her while she pulled them on. Then he yanked his own jeans on, ignoring his lack of underwear, and tugged the gray sweatshirt over his head. He stuffed the blue swim trunks in his pocket.

"I guess you're right," he said, and his voice was sad. "It's time to go."

He gathered all the supplies he'd brought and loaded them in the boat, and it seemed only minutes before they were heading across the dark water to the mainland.

She held the light the way he asked, and once she turned to stare over her shoulder at the island, but she could barely make it out in the growing darkness.

It floated, a dark, ethereal mound imposed upon a pewter lake under a star-studded night sky.

The trip home on the motorcycle was more than a little frightening. Surrounded by inky blackness, the bike roared around curves and up and down hills, and she couldn't see more than a few feet ahead. She could only trust that Ben knew what he was doing. She felt exposed and helpless.

Even though Ben patted her hand now and then in a reassuring way, it did nothing to dispel the feeling of absolute aloneness, of vulnerability, that mushroomed inside her.

At her apartment, he kissed her good-night—a lingering kiss that she couldn't return. She was exhausted, and she didn't want to think about the events of the day. She didn't want to think at all. She wanted to put her head in a hole like an ostrich and pretend the world had disappeared.

"I'll call you in the morning," Ben promised.

"Don't," she heard herself say. "I won't be in the office. I have to go look at some property."

It wasn't true, but she knew it was a necessary lie. She was going to have to distance herself from him, and she ought to start right now.

"I'll be in touch soon, then." There was a firmness in his words that she couldn't bring herself to argue with.

She dragged herself inside, too tired to think or feel, and dropped her clothing on the floor. She fell into bed and drew the covers up to her nose. Sleep came instantly.

SHE WAS SLUMPED AT HER desk the next morning in a state of shock, remembering in vivid detail exactly what she'd done the day before with Ben. She was trying to figure out what she'd do the next time she saw him, when there was a call from her bank manager, Nigel Forbes.

Nigel was a forty-five-year-old refugee from two failed marriages, only now beginning to even suspect that perhaps some of the problems he'd had with women might have originated with him.

After a barrage of invitations, Annabelle had gone out with him once, and the first fifteen minutes of that date confirmed what she'd suspected all along: Nigel Forbes was a self-absorbed, egocentric bore. He'd nearly put her to sleep talking about investment schemes and registered retirement savings plans and how clever he was at his job.

He cleared his throat now and said in a ponderous tone, "Annabelle, there's a slight problem with your business account this morning. A check is in from Hopman and Cook. It came in Friday, and there aren't enough funds in the account to cover it. I realize Cyril usually handles these matters, but he wasn't available when I called Friday and he's not there again this morning."

Hopman and Cook were the lawyers for Midas Realty and Pinetree Developments. Annabelle had written the legal firm a sizable check the week before to cover their fees on the complicated closing of a condo she'd sold.

She frowned. "Sorry, Nigel. I was sure there was enough in that account to cover. I must have miscalculated. What about the overdraft?"

"It's the overdraft I'm talking about, Annabelle."

Shock waves rippled through her. The automatic overdraft protection on the business account was generous. How on earth had the account dropped by that much? She and Cyril shared the task of keeping a close eye on the ledgers, although he'd taken on more of the responsibility during the past few months while she'd been so preoccupied with the development deal.

"Cy's due back early this afternoon. Do you want to wait and talk to him?"

"Actually, Annabelle," Nigel's deep voice went on ponderously, "this is something we really ought to discuss immediately. Are you by any chance free for lunch?"

The absolutely last thing she wanted to do today was meet Nigel Forbes for lunch.

"I'm sorry, Nigel, I have to . . ."

"I'm afraid it's rather urgent, Annabelle."

He *was* her banker, and if it was urgent, it had to be about money. Apprehension sent a tiny chill down her back, and after a moment, as cheerfully as she could manage, she said, "I'll just cancel this meeting I have, then. Will one o'clock be all right?"

"One is fine. I'll come by and pick you up. We'll go to my club. Oh, and Annabelle, could you possibly bring along your list of receivables for the last sixty days?"

She agreed and hung up slowly, aware that her hand was trembling.

**7**

"CY, I'M SO GLAD YOU'RE back. Could I talk to you for a minute?"

Without waiting for an answer, Annabelle followed her partner down the hall and closed his office door firmly behind them. She threw the file folder with the accounts receivable down on his desktop and sank into an overstuffed leather chair, drawing in a deep breath, incredibly relieved that there was someone to share her concern.

She'd returned from her upsetting lunch with Nigel an hour before, and she'd been watching for Cyril to come back to the office ever since.

"What's up, partner? You're looking a little frazzled around the edges." Cy raised his thick eyebrows at her and tipped his chair back. He folded his hands behind his head, propping his feet in their usual spot on his desktop. There were wide sweat stains under the sleeves of his blue cotton shirt.

"Thank God that guy finally fixed the air-conditioning in here." He sighed. "It's an oven outside. My neck got burned just in the time I was out of the car. Hey, you look like you got a few rays yourself over the weekend, Annabelle. Went to the beach, huh?"

"Yes. No. Not the beach."

She'd gotten far more sun than she needed, but she wasn't about to tell Cy how or where. Her nose and chin were as red as stoplights, her freckles were reproducing, and various other parts of her anatomy stung painfully under her clothing. But sunburn wasn't the thing she needed to talk about at the moment.

"Cy, what on earth's going on with our bank accounts? I just had lunch with Nigel Forbes. He said the business account was seriously overdrawn. He practically ordered me to bring him a list of our receivables, and then he sat there with a pocket calculator and . . . and added and subtracted and mumbled under his breath and shook his head for over an hour."

She'd had the almost-overwhelming urge to pick up her plate of seafood lasagna and dump it right over Nigel's meticulously combed sandy hair. He could at least have waited until they'd finished eating. As it was, he'd made her so nervous and so angry she'd barely tasted any of her food.

Her voice trembled now with both outrage at Nigel and alarm at what he'd discovered. She struggled to control it. "Anyway, Cy, he came to the conclusion that some of the receivables are coming in late, and that one deposit for twenty-three thousand is totally missing, on a deal I was sure Johnny closed two weeks ago. I asked him and he said he gave you the check to deposit."

Cy frowned, bushy eyebrows meeting on his forehead. He lowered his arms and lifted his legs from the desktop, pulling the chair in closer and leaning across to take Annabelle's hand in his own. He patted it in a fatherly fashion, and she felt comforted even though nothing had really changed.

"Look, kid, offhand I can't tell you what this is all about because I don't know, but I do know there's nothing to get in a panic about. I've been keeping a running tab on our accounts receivable, and there should have been more than enough to cover our outflow. There seems to have been some kind of glitch. Don't worry, I'll straighten it out right away. I'm sorry I wasn't here and you had to go through all this with Nigel. He's such a panic button when it comes to money, you know that. Now why don't you just leave it with me? I'll talk to Johnny. Maybe the check got mislaid or something. The last thing you need right now is something else to be concerned over." Cyril gave her a reassuring wink. "You just concentrate on getting your hands on Likely Cove, and let old Cy take care of the small stuff, okay?"

*Concentrate on getting the cove.*

Annabelle remembered the day before, and her stomach tightened, just the way it had each time she allowed herself to think about those hours spent on Paradise. She was pitifully grateful that Cy had no idea she'd spent all of Sunday with Ben, and that she'd spent maybe ten minutes discussing business before giving up any hope of ever talking Ben into selling them the cove.

As for the problems with the bank, Cy's casual attitude comforted her. Of course, he'd know if there was something seriously wrong. Of course, Nigel was just being ridiculous about this.

She could already feel some of the tension leave her shoulders and arms. She got up and bent over, pressing a quick kiss on Cy's cheek. "Thanks, partner. What would I ever do without you?"

"God knows. I'm indispensable. I'm glad you realize it." The sound of Cy's easy laughter followed her all the way down the hall and into her own office. There was a ton of work waiting for her—things she'd put aside the week before.

She switched on her computer and for the next two hours, she tried her best to dream up irresistible blurbs for the new listings Midas would advertise the following week in the *Real Estate News*.

"Lakefront property, private beach . . ."

Real-estate ads had never before struck her as even faintly erotic, but now her brain clicked up seductive images of her and Ben, naked on the beach at Paradise. She ought to be appalled by her behavior there, but the sensual memories overwhelmed any saner reactions.

"Spacious rooms, Jacuzzi tub in master bedroom . . ."

What would it be like to share a Jacuzzi with him? To make love in a queen-size bed? She remembered his clever hands and the way he used them; his mouth, the tickle of his mustache on her belly, the way he shuddered when . . .

"Annabelle? Hey, Earth to Annabelle."

Startled, feeling as if Johnny could guess where her mind had been, she jumped to attention and felt herself flush crimson.

He stood in her office doorway studying her, head tipped to one side. "Boy, you really got a touch of the sun on the weekend. You're as red as a lobster." He crossed his arms over his chest and leaned back against the doorframe. "So how's it going? Any progress on getting Likely Cove? You been in touch with that Baxter guy again?"

She wished to God her partners could talk about something else today.

"I'm working on it," she lied. She'd have to tell them the truth soon—that it was hopeless—but for now, she didn't have the energy. She groped for a topic of conversation that would get him off Likely Cove, or Ben Baxter.

"Did you have a good weekend? It was your weekend with Gillian, wasn't it?" Like most fathers, his daughter was a favorite subject.

Johnny nodded. "Yeah, supposed to be, but Caroline wanted to take her to Vancouver to buy school clothes this weekend. I'm going to pick them both up at the airport in an hour, then Gillian's spending the week at my place. Caroline has a seminar on personal development she's attending all this week."

He unfolded his arms and came into her office, leaning on the back of a chair, a pleading expression in his dark brown eyes.

"Which is why I need you to fill in for me on my open house at Glenmeadows tonight, Annabelle. I'd really like to take Gillian out for a burger and maybe to a movie. I haven't seen the kid all week. What d'ya say?"

What she ought to say was no, she knew that. "How come you guys consider your free time more valuable than mine, anyway?"

"Hey, that's not it at all. It's just that Caroline throws these curves at me all the time, changing the times when I'm supposed to have my kid."

Exasperated, Annabelle wondered when Johnny was going to finally stop allowing his ex-wife to control his life . . . and, inadvertently, hers. With regularity, Annabelle found herself rearranging her own plans to accommodate still another crisis in Johnny's personal life. Granted, he always made it up to her in one way or another, but she resented it.

"Johnny, I don't think so. I went to that meeting for you last week, and I'd really planned on having an early night tonight. And besides, my car's in the garage getting painted."

She'd taken it in first thing this morning, to have the scratches Ben's dog had inflicted repainted.

"No problem, I'll pay for a cab. And you won't be out late. You only have to be there for two hours, seven till nine. Please, Annabelle?" Johnny had a little-boy sort of charm that was hard to resist.

Well, what the heck. She could ride her bike over and get some exercise while she was at it. She might as well be sitting at some open house. If she was at her apartment, she'd just be waiting for Ben to phone, even though she really didn't want to talk with him today. At least, she was pretty sure she didn't. Doing something might take her mind off—

"Ben?" She gaped at the doorway as if she'd conjured him up just by thinking about him.

"Hi, I hope I'm not interrupting anything important?"

He filled the doorway of her office, his large body making Johnny look downright puny by comparison, and she'd always considered Johnny a big man. Until now.

"I had some business in town," he went on, "and I needed to talk to you, so I thought I'd drop by." He moved farther into the room and held out a hand to Johnny.

"I'm Ben Baxter. How do you do?"

"Johnny Calvados, pleased to meet you. I'm Annabelle's partner. One of them." He shook Ben's hand. "The junior one," he added with a laugh. "And I was just leaving. Annabelle, maybe let me know for sure about the open house before you leave for the day, all right?" He hurried out the door, making a point of closing it after himself.

"Mind if I sit down?" Without waiting for an answer, Ben sank into the red leather chair and propped one knee across the other. He was nonchalant and casual, and all she could think of was how he'd looked naked. She hoped to God her sunburn masked the flush spreading up her throat and face.

"I tried to call you earlier, Bella, but your receptionist said you were out for lunch."

The intimacy of the pet name, of his tone of voice, made her flush even deeper. "Yes, I had a, umm, a business lunch. With my banker." Now why did she feel she had to tell him that? Why was her heart hammering, her hands trembling, her knees rubbery all of a sudden? Why did this man have such a disturbing effect on her?

Granted, he looked spectacular. He had on a white cotton shirt that made his tan look exotic. He wore the usual snug-fitting denims, and his boots looked as though they'd just been polished. The smile he gave her was intimate, and she felt absurdly shy.

"I have a big favor to ask of you," he began, after a moment of silence.

"What is it?" She sat back in her chair and tried hard to appear cool, confident, in control—but without a shred of success.

Ben seemed a bit uncomfortable himself now. "You met my friend Jason Collins, when you were out at the trailer."

She nodded, a little apprehensive as to what he was going to ask. Teenage boys weren't exactly her area of expertise; in fact, she knew nothing whatsoever about them. Except that they made her nervous.

"Well, his mother, Daisy, just lost her job. She's been working at a bottling plant and it closed down. She's a single parent, and now she wants to get into something that has a future—something with the potential to earn her and Jase a better living."

"Like real estate?"

He smiled at her. "You're quick. Yeah. Like real estate. See, Daisy's sort of impulsive, and I'd hate to see her jump into this before she has a clear idea of what's involved. She's done a good job raising Jason, but money's a big problem. They're not well-off, and she'd have to mortgage her place in order to get the money for the real-estate course. So before she does that, I wondered if maybe you'd talk to her, give her an honest picture of what's involved here."

"Of course, I will. Tell her to come in and see me—"

"Actually, I wondered if maybe you'd come out to Oyama and meet her?" His voice was tentative.

Annabelle opened her mouth to protest, but Ben was already talking.

"In fact, I thought maybe you could come out tonight, as soon as you're finished work. I can wait for you. We're having a barbecue at my place—Daisy and Jase and a few of the other neighbors—and I thought it would be a good chance for you to meet Daisy on a sort of casual basis."

Alarm bells went off in her head. She was incapable of being around Ben and staying rational—she'd learned that yesterday. She hadn't had a chance even to sit down and figure out what she was doing with him. And last night, she'd made a firm resolve to stay away from him.

Hadn't she? She groped for an excuse. "I can't come tonight, Ben. My car's being repaired."

"The damage my dog did, right? Send me the bill. I'll pay."

"My insurance is covering it."

"Then the least I can do is give you dinner." He glanced at his watch. "It's already after five, you must be ready to leave for the day. I'll drive you out to Oyama on the bike. It's parked right outside. And if you don't want to ride back on the motorcycle in the dark, then I'll bring you home in the truck. Promise."

She felt her resistance begin to slip.

"Please, Bella." His expression was pleading. "I'd really like you to talk to Daisy. I'm concerned about her and Jason."

She thought of the sandwich she'd probably eat while sitting alone, bored out of her skull for two hours at Johnny's open house. She thought of how often her partners took advantage of her free time, and rebellion rose up in her. "Okay. I'll just turn this computer off and we'll go," she heard herself say.

Ben looked as surprised as she felt at her sudden capitulation.

"I'll have to stop off at my apartment and change, though. This dress isn't designed for riding on the back of a motorcycle. And I have to talk to Johnny before I leave." She felt not one shred of guilt at forcing Johnny to attend his own open house.

Ten minutes later she climbed on the bike behind Ben as if she'd been straddling motorcycles all her life, tucked her dress recklessly high on her thighs and propped her elegant high heels on the foot pegs. As they roared out of the parking lot, she looked back and giggled at the stunned and incredulous expressions on both Cy's and Johnny's faces as they stared after her.

WITH THE HELP OF HIS friends several summers before, Ben had built a barbecue pit behind his trailer, angling two levels of decking into the natural slope of the hillside. Rico's wife, Tilley, was a genius at landscaping, and she'd planted flowers and shrubs all around the decks.

Ben had put in apricot trees so that there was plenty of shade. He'd made a pond off to one side, damming the creek and allowing it to pool in a rock-lined hollow and then run out again on its natural course down the mountainside.

The problem was, the ducks and geese fought viciously over the pond. At the moment, there was a noisy full-scale war going on, not ten feet from the group gathered on the decks.

The idyllic summer evening was further marred by the proximity of the llama pen. Cupid and Clara had their necks stuck through the slats and were ogling everyone with big, surprised eyes and making their usual humming sounds. They looked and sounded like innocent voyeurs at an X-rated peep show, fascinated and horrified in equal measure.

Annabelle felt like that herself. Ben's friends were slightly overwhelming.

"Hey, Benjie, you're late to your own party," Rico had greeted them when they arrived. "I put the steaks on already. I'm starving." He'd come lumbering over from the barbecue, battered straw hat covering his bald head, acres of plaid shorts stretched across his expanded paunch. "Tilley's inside doing something to the potato salad. And who's this luscious creature?" He'd bent in a courtly bow and kissed Annabelle's hand while Ben introduced him.

"Don't be overwhelmed by Rico. He's nothing but a fast-talking Lothario," a tall, wiry man called Amos advised, handing Annabelle a glass of wine. "Here's his better half, now. She keeps him in line. Tilley, meet Annabelle."

A tiny woman wearing a yellow flowered sundress on her pencil-thin form marched around the corner, and everyone pretended to snap to attention. Rico even saluted.

"Come over here with me, Annabelle, and let these men get on with cooking steaks." Tilley's salt-and-pepper hair hung down her back in a single long, thick braid. "I used to be a schoolteacher. It comes in handy now and then, dealing with this lot." Energy seemed to radiate from her in waves. "Ben, go slice those tomatoes, and the salad needs tossing. Leroy, bring us each a glass of wine, if you please. Jason, go scrub those filthy hands and put some of those tortilla chips I left on the counter into the basket that's on the table and pass them around. Now, my dear, sit here in the shade beside me—that lounge chair is comfortable—and tell me how you ever got talked into riding on the back of Ben Baxter's motorcycle."

Annabelle, feeling about seven years old, did as she was told.

BEN HOVERED NEARBY until he was certain Annabelle felt relaxed. She was soon sipping her wine and laughing at Tilley's nonsense. He knew that his friends would take Annabelle into their midst and make her feel like part of an extended, if slightly batty, family, and he was grateful.

He was worried about her, and he needed all the help he could get. He'd felt her draw away from him the day before, right after they'd made love. Just about the time he'd thought all the barriers were down, she'd gone remote and cool on him again.

Which showed how complex a personality she was, and that made her all the more intriguing. He was going to have to go slow and easy with her, tough as that would be. He'd spent most of the previous night worrying that because he'd let things get out of hand between them, she'd dump him flat and never agree to go anywhere with him again. It scared the living hell out of him, which was why he'd called on everyone this morning for help. He'd come to the conclusion that being part of a group wouldn't be as intimidating for her as going out alone with him.

Daisy had lost her job, all right. But she'd never thought of real estate until he'd suggested it a few hours ago. Fortunately she wasn't opposed to the idea, especially after he offered to pay for the course if she'd go along with him and just ask Annabelle some logical questions.

Not that he'd ever known Daisy to be logical, but in desperate times a man had to use whatever was available.

His pride had taken a licking. Amos and Rico were never going to let him forget that he'd actually had to ask them for assistance where a woman was concerned. The reprobates had even demanded sirloin steaks in return for showing up tonight.

And the whole plan had worked, because she was here, wasn't she?

Right now, he had a dozen things he ought to do, but he stood and looked at Annabelle anyway—at the way her full mouth tilted into a wide, crooked smile at something Tilley said. He loved looking at her, loved the way her long fingers curled around her glass, the way she held her head, the way her legs curved gracefully into those intriguing wide-legged white shorts.

What was it about this particular woman that made him feel warm and protective and exhilarated and aroused and clumsy all at the same time?

Musky perfume engulfed him and a feminine kiss landed somewhere in the vicinity of his ear, while a husky voice almost as deep as his own purred, "Hey, Ben, darlin', how's it going?"

Daisy Collins winked up at him and bumped him in a friendly fashion with her hip, then swore as the bowl she was holding tipped and juice dribbled out, staining the magenta jumpsuit that fit her generous curves like a second skin.

"Damn, would you look at that, now. I'm worse than Jason at getting myself in a mess. Here, hold this." She handed Ben the dripping bowl and swabbed at herself with a tissue. "Sorry I'm late. I had to go to the unemployment office and fill in forms this afternoon. It nearly drove me to suicide, but I decided not to do anything drastic—it's not fair to saddle you with Jason now that he's a teenager. So don't say I never did you a favor. I swear they delight in making ordinary people feel like nerds down there. Should we put this fruit salad in the fridge, or are we ready to eat? Hey, is *that* the lady you're trying to impress over there with Tilley? *She's* the real-estate person you want me to play twenty questions with? Whoa, Ben, this one's got class. You're heading up in the world. Now, if you'd just get yourself a respectable job while you're finding one for me . . ."

ANNABELLE SAW THE breathtakingly beautiful girl with the long mass of inky black, curly hair flirting with Ben. She pretended not to watch, but inside her stomach she felt a sensation very much like jealousy. She tried to listen to Tilley, but she knew the exact moment when Ben and the woman disappeared together around the front of the trailer.

It felt like several hours before they reappeared, and she tried hard to paste on a friendly smile when Ben led the seductive creature straight over to her.

"Annabelle, I'd like you to meet Daisy Collins, Jason's mother."

Daisy Collins didn't look old enough to be out of high school, much less the mother of a teenager. She had a body that a model might envy, a smile that inspired one in return, and eyes as clear and green as lake water.

Her deep, throaty voice worked overtime, Annabelle soon learned. Daisy was a talker.

"It's super to meet you, Annabelle. Ben says you won't mind if I ask you a *billion* and one questions about real estate. God, I *love* your hair. Where d'you get it cut? Hey, Tilley, how's the gardening going? I wish you'd hustle over to my place and tell me what the heck I should do with that front border. The hibiscus I put in died and the whole thing looks like a bomb site now."

Barely pausing to draw breath, she rattled on, "Annabelle, I guess Ben told you about me losing my job. What d'ya figure? You think I have a hope in hell of making it selling real estate?"

Annabelle opened her mouth to answer, but Rico interrupted.

"Ladies and gentlemen." He'd made a megaphone out of a piece of cardboard. "The steaks are now ready. I repeat, the steaks are now ready and in danger of disappearing fast, so come and get yours."

Ben was suddenly at Annabelle's side with a plate.

"These people are world-class eaters. Let's get you at least one helping before it's too late." He guided her over to the table he and Rico had constructed out of two sawhorses and a piece of plywood, and he piled salad and buns and baked potatoes on her plate until Annabelle begged him to stop.

"Annabelle, you busy next weekend?" Amos didn't wait for her answer. "Rico and I are the organizers for Lake Country Days, and we've nominated you as judge for the parade on Saturday. You'll be sure she turns up, won't you, Ben?"

"But I'm...I'm not sure.... I mean, I've never judged...I couldn't possibly..."

Amos waved away her objections as if they were mosquitoes.

"Nothing to it. Tilley's arranging the whole thing. Her and Ben'll fill you in on what to do, right, Ben? Judging starts at eight sharp out in front of the Winfield Rec Center."

"Eight? Oh, that's much too early for me. I'd have to allow half an hour to drive out from Kelowna, and—"

"Don't even have to bother with breakfast. You can have all the pancakes you can eat. Judges eat free at the Pancake Jubilee," he said, raking his hand through his shock of thick gray hair.

Amos sounded as if he were awarding her the keys to the city. "It'll only take an hour or two. Rest of the day you can have all to yourself."

Ben shrugged when she turned to him for help. "I'm afraid I can't get you out of this, Bella. I've already been nominated for three separate jobs myself, including judging the parade. Far as I know, nothing on earth works as an excuse once Amos gets an idea in his head." He guided her to a chair beside a rickety card table and set his overflowing plate down beside hers. "Besides, it'll be fun. Lake Country Days is a sort of community birthday party held every summer out here in the boonies. It's a mixture of events—races, ball games, pancake breakfast, kids' events. The whole thing starts with the parade. I'll pick you up on Saturday morning at seven if you like."

Annabelle shook her head. "I'll have to bring my own car in case I have to go back to town on business. I've got several properties listed in the *Real Estate News*, and Saturday and Sunday can be busy days."

"You'll be able to come to the dance with me that evening, though, won't you? Saturday night there's always a big dance. Amos has me in charge of the hall, but apart from keeping an eye on the bar and seeing things are cleaned up afterward, I'll have lots of time to waltz with you."

"It's been years since I waltzed. I'll step all over your feet." But the thought of dancing with Ben was captivating.

"I'll wear my boots. It won't hurt me a bit." His smile was charming, and the look he gave her spread warmth through every bone in her body.

What was it about him that made her feel pretty and young and sexy each time she was with him?

She gave in and agreed to judge the parade.

# 8

FOR THE NEXT SEVERAL hours, Annabelle ate, drank wine, listened, talked, laughed, and thoroughly enjoyed Ben's friends.

And every minute of those hours, she was aware that Ben was nearby, quietly refilling her glass, bringing her dessert, filling her in on details she didn't understand about the fast-paced conversation that flowed around her. Their eyes met often, and he'd smile or wink in intimate acknowledgment of her.

It was after nine by the time everyone left, calling out friendly insults as they drove down the driveway.

There was very little cleaning up to do; Tilley had organized a cleanup squad and bossed everyone unmercifully, so everything was very much in order.

Ben made a fresh pot of coffee, and together they carried mugs outside to watch the last of the sunset on the lakes far below.

They slouched side by side in lawn chairs, and Annabelle kicked off her sandals and sighed with contentment, aware that she was relaxed and just a tiny bit tipsy from all the wine she'd drunk.

"I really like your friends, Ben. I'm glad you asked me to come tonight. They're . . . different . . . from the people I know in Kelowna."

He grunted. "Nuttier, you mean. It must be the air out here."

"They're easygoing. Friendly." She remembered Rico doing a slow dance with a broomstick. "A little zany, maybe." She sipped her coffee and smiled at the memory of several spirited and ribald comments Rico and Amos had made to Ben when they thought she wasn't listening.

"Daisy is nothing short of spectacular." All evening, she'd been wondering about Daisy and Ben. "Did...did you and Daisy ever . . . Well, she's so beautiful, I could certainly see any man being attracted.... I mean, it's none of my business, but . . ." She felt stupid for asking, but some part of her insisted she had to know.

"Did we ever have an affair?" Ben shook his head. "Nope. Not even close. Jason tried to set us up a few times, but there're no sparks there at all. Never were."

Annabelle was shocked. "Jason? Set you up with his mother?"

"Sure. The kid looks up to me, and I guess he figured it would solve a lot of problems if Daisy and I got together. But she's always seemed more like a sister to me." His voice grew somber. "A real problem sister at times. She has a knack for getting involved with the wrong sort of men. The last one was a real prize—knocked her around. Like most men who beat on women, he was also a coward, so when he got a bit of his own medicine, he cleared out." Ben's expression became grim, and Annabelle caught a glimpse of a very different person than the easygoing man she thought she knew.

"She's lucky to have you as a friend."

He turned to her and his warm smile was back in place. "We all need good friends, Annabelle."

She cradled her coffee and thought about that. Seeing Ben with his friends tonight had made her poignantly aware of how lonely her own life was. Cy and Johnny were business partners and friends, but she doubted she'd call on either of them if she needed help in her personal life.

Ben reached over and took her hand, holding it lightly in his. "It was generous of you to invite Daisy to come to the office and watch what goes on. I appreciate it."

Annabelle grinned. "It wasn't entirely altruistic. I can't wait to see Johnny and Cy turn into gibbering idiots when they lay eyes on her. But she'll find out that real estate can be very difficult at times, and she needs to understand that before she decides to pursue it."

For the first time all evening, she remembered the upsetting day she'd had. "You and your friends certainly took my mind off the problems at the office, anyway," she mused.

"What problems are those, Annabelle?" His voice was lazy and gentle, inviting confidence. His fingers and hers were now interlaced, and it gave her an absurd sense of security.

"Oh, just some problems with the bank." She hadn't meant to say anything about it, but it seemed easy to confide in Ben.

"Cash-flow problems—the kind any business has once in a while, I guess." She frowned and shook her head. "Except that the money should have been in the account. I don't understand it."

"What money's that?"

Impulsively, she explained about the large deposit that seemed to be missing. "Cy said he'd look into it, but I mean to ask Johnny about it again myself. I don't understand how that amount of money could get misplaced, do you?"

"Has it ever happened before?"

She shook her head. "Not that I know of. Cy keeps a close eye on our accounts, just as I do. There must be a logical explanation for all this." She looked over at him and found him studying her intently. "I'm sorry, Ben. I'm boring you with all this business stuff."

"Not at all. It helps to talk to an outsider sometimes, gives you a new slant on what's going on. And if I can help at all, you'll ask, won't you, Annabelle?"

She thought of Likely Cove, and of how very much he could help her if he only would. But she didn't tell him so.

"I think it's time for me to go home," she said instead, wondering if he'd suggest something else . . . and wondering, too, what she'd do if he did.

But he set his mug on the ground and reached for her shoes. He took her foot in his hand, cradling it for a moment before he fitted it into her strappy sandal and fastened it, sending arrows of delight coursing up her legs at the sensation of his strong fingers on her bare skin. He put her other sandal on in the same way and then stood, reaching down to pull her up beside him.

"We'll take the truck. Just wait here and I'll get it out of the garage."

They chatted on the ride home about the barbecue, laughing together about things Rico or Amos had said or done, and all the while she wondered if he was planning to make love to her.

At her door he kissed her—a nice kiss, but hardly passionate.

She thought of inviting him in, but before she could form the words, he said, "See ya soon. Thanks again for helping Daisy."

With that, he turned and walked away, and she stood at her door, half expecting him to come back, until she heard his truck drive off.

She went in and slammed the door as hard as she could.

Damn Ben Baxter, anyhow! He'd somehow invaded her life and turned its careful, controlled pattern upside down. He'd sneaked in behind her defenses and made her want him—a bold physical ache that his lovemaking had ignited and which refused to be doused by common sense or reason. And then tonight he didn't even bother to kiss her properly.

When she finally fell asleep, the dreams she had were X-rated, but the physical responses the dream Ben roused in her feverish body did nothing to slake the desire that burned within her.

IT TOOK EVERY OUNCE of self-control he could muster to turn and walk away from her that evening, but Ben had a gut feeling that pushing Annabelle now wouldn't be in his best interests in the long run.

And it was the long run he was interested in here. He knew that for certain, now.

On the drive home, he thought about the evening. The best part had been after everyone had left, he decided, when he and she were alone, discussing the party, sharing coffee while the last of the evening light faded from the sky. He'd had a sense of completeness then, of homecoming, a feeling that he wanted the twilight to go on and on. He'd kept wanting to kiss her, to make love to her, and he'd kept resisting, difficult as it was. He didn't want to rush her again, scare her off, because Annabelle was a woman he wanted both in and out of his bed.

So, was he thinking "permanent" here?

Ben followed the winding highway around the lakes and up the long hills to Oyama, pondering that question. Until recently, he'd never given much thought to marrying again.

His ex-wife Sharon had pretty much cured him of the marriage bug. They'd lasted six years, during which time she'd graduated from law school and started making waves as a criminal lawyer. It had taken them both that long to figure out that marriage to an unambitious cop wasn't fitting in with her plans.

He'd loved her, and it had taken him a long time to get over her. It wasn't an experience he was eager to repeat.

But Annabelle wasn't Sharon. He was older now. He'd be certain before he committed himself that she understood that what she saw was what she got, that he wasn't ever going to write a bestseller or become the prime minister of Canada—or even put on a business suit and commute to Kelowna every day.

*And what made him think she'd want him, with or without a business suit?*

Well, she was physically drawn to him, as he was to her. God, he could hardly keep his hands off her. Whoever said that getting older made a guy less horny?

But there was a great deal of Annabelle hidden behind a barbed-wire fence—a part of her that she hadn't revealed to him yet.

She was beginning to open up more, though. Tonight she'd talked about her business problems in a way that made him feel she trusted him.

He thought about what she'd said about the bank and frowned. Large deposits didn't just get mislaid. Somebody was playing cute with the money, that was pretty certain. It was obvious Annabelle trusted these bozos she worked with implicitly, but that didn't convince Ben they were honest.

In fact, it mightn't hurt a bit to look a little deeper into Cyril Lisk and Johnny Calvados.

He pulled into his yard and shut off the truck's engine. He had nothing to do this week that couldn't be done next; he might just as well play detective.

He got out, failed to convince Susie that his face didn't need a thorough washing, and checked that Cupid and Clara were safely in their pen before he went into the trailer.

Clara was due to have a baby soon now, but she carried high under her rib cage and her pregnancy was well disguised by her long, fluffy hair.

His animals had been all the company he needed, most of the time.

Funny how lonely the place seemed all of a sudden.

DAISY ARRIVED AT THE office at nine in the morning the day after the barbecue. Her mass of dark hair was drawn back into a businesslike chignon. She wore a red camisole underneath a blue denim suit-jacket, and the matching short denim skirt bared yards of shapely thigh and calf.

Her effect on Cy and Johnny was every bit as dramatic as Annabelle had anticipated. They each found a dozen excuses to visit Annabelle's office that morning.

At ten, Johnny even made a pot of herbal tea—Daisy had said she preferred herbal tea to coffee—and brought it to them, complete with sugared doughnuts.

"He's kinda sweet," Daisy commented after he'd reluctantly left them alone. She poured two cups and handed Annabelle one. "Guess he doesn't understand what sugar can do to your body, though."

"I don't think it's sugar affecting him this morning. You have a devastating effect on men, Daisy. You must know that."

Daisy nodded and sighed, as if it was a cross in life she had to bear. "I have a tough time figuring out who the good guys are, though. You, now, you're lucky, having Ben. He's a good guy, definitely."

Annabelle opened her mouth to assure Daisy that she didn't by any stretch of the imagination "have" Ben, but Daisy was already three sentences ahead.

"See, Ben's a winner in my books. I don't know what I'd have done with that kid of mine when he got in all that trouble a couple years ago if Ben hadn't been there for him." She shook her head. "Jase got in with a bad crowd, and I was working lots of overtime right then. Anyway, he started doing some drugs, stealing to get money."

Her lovely face grew somber, and in her eyes was re-membered anguish. "Ben straightened him out. He's been sort of like a big brother to Jase ever since." Daisy broke off a piece of doughnut and stuck it in her mouth, chewing and talking at the same time.

"Wouldn't think a confirmed bachelor like Ben would want a kid hanging around all the time, what with his lady friends and all—" She stopped and rolled her eyes. "Gag me—me and my big mouth. I'm talking about *before* here. And anyway, Ben never overlaps. Trust me on this. If he's taking you out, then he won't be seeing anybody else, guaranteed. But he's had women swarming all over him in the past. I'm sure that's no news to you. I mean, he's got that simply great bod, he's real good-looking, and he's got a good soul, as well. Heck, I don't need to tell you that."

Annabelle swallowed hard. "Of course. I mean, of course not."

Daisy was off again. "You know, sometimes me and the guys give him a hard time about not having a real job and all?" Daisy widened her eyes. "We all tease him a lot about being unemployed. But Ben could make a small fortune if he wanted, just with his wine alone. It's won prizes at local tastings, and that winery, Inglenook, well, they asked him several times if he'd sell to them, but he won't. He says making wine's his hobby, and if he started doing it for money, it would take all the joy out of it. Doesn't that just give you back faith in the whole male species?"

Annabelle wasn't sure. She was astonished that Ben would turn down what might be a lucrative business offer. She knew of Inglenook wines; they'd gained an international reputation in the last few years, selling not only in North America but abroad, as well.

It irked her that Ben would casually turn down what could prove to be a lucrative business opportunity; she was a businesswoman, desperately struggling to make her company successful against monumental odds. It seemed he'd been offered success demanding little effort on his part, and he wouldn't even accept it.

Johnny stuck his head in the doorway. "Daisy, I have to go down to the registry office and search this title. It might be a good opportunity for you to see how it's done." He looked as anxious as Annabelle had ever seen him look, waiting for Daisy to answer.

"Super, let's go."

Annabelle thought Johnny might be about to faint with pleasure as he escorted Daisy out the door.

She settled down to do paperwork, telling herself what a relief it was not to have Daisy chattering away and distracting her.

But she found herself thinking of a dozen questions to ask about Ben the next time Daisy happened to get on the subject. It was shameful of her, taking advantage of the other woman's openness that way, but she couldn't resist.

Ben had somehow become the focus of her thoughts, the central theme that played through her mind at all hours of the day and night. She still spent agonizing moments worrying about the September deadline with the investors and the disturbing money situation the companies were experiencing, but the summer had also taken on a slow-motion dreamlike quality that made September seem nebulous and far away.

DECIDING WHAT TO WEAR to judge the parade on Saturday became a lot easier after Daisy suggested Annabelle bring a dress along for the dance and change at her place.

"You'll have to have a shower anyhow, maybe even two or three. It's always boiling hot for Lake Country Days. The joke is that Tilley insists on good weather and God's scared to refuse. I always wear as little as I can legally get away with during the day, myself," Daisy remarked casually.

Daisy's theory of partial nudity definitely had merit, Annabelle concluded by noon on Saturday. She was wearing shorts, a sleeveless top and a wide-brimmed straw hat, but she was sure she was melting. The judging and the pancake breakfast were over, and the temperature was already breaking all records.

That morning, Ben had guided her through the complexities of judging, which turned out to be a lot of fun. Jason was in the parade, dressed in a serape and a huge sombrero, leading Ben's llama, Cupid. What made the judging entertaining was having Ben beside her, making outrageous remarks, giving her a poker-faced but hilarious commentary on certain civic-minded and stuffy officials, and being unashamedly partisan in his judging of Jason and Cupid.

"It's my hat as well as my llama. Damned right, Jase ought to get first prize," he argued when Annabelle took him to task.

There were a dozen judges, and Ben was as elated as Jason when the boy did win a red ribbon.

He came racing over to them when the parade was over, ecstatic with both his ribbon and the twenty-dollar prize that went with it. He and Ben exchanged a complicated handshake and a victory yell.

"I LEFT CUPID OVER THERE in the shade. I tied him to a tree and gave him a drink. See where he is? That guy standing beside him says he wants to talk to you about maybe buying some alpacas, Ben. Hey, here comes Mom. Guess what, Mom, I won first prize for best interpretation with a pet. Twenty dollars—look!"

Daisy, dressed in shorts and a brief halter top, seemed oblivious to the fact that she was the focus of admiring male glances. She shoved her huge sunglasses up to her forehead, inspected the ribbon as if she'd never seen one before, and gave Jason a congratulatory thump on the arm. "Way to go, Jase. I'm really proud of you, kid."

Ben wandered over to talk to the alpaca man, and Jason turned to the women. "You two want a hot dog and a drink? My treat. I got enough money for all of us."

Annabelle was about to refuse, but Daisy smiled at her son and said, "Yeah, please. That would be fabulous, Jase. A hot dog, loaded, and a diet cola. Same for Annabelle."

He ran off to the snack table.

"Really, Daisy, he shouldn't be spending his money on me," Annabelle objected. She was well aware Jason and his mother didn't exactly have an overabundance of money.

Daisy was watching her son, her pride in him making her lovely face glow. "He's a generous kid, and he's practicing to be a man. When he offers things of his own free will, it's a good idea to accept. Some guys never learn that giving feels good, y'know," she added. "All they know how to do is take. I don't want Jase to be that kind of a man."

Annabelle was touched, and very impressed with Daisy's insight. She was beginning to suspect that appearances were deceiving; the brassy young woman was a good and thoughtful mother to her son, and a razor-sharp mind hid behind the frivolous exterior Daisy chose to present to the world.

"What d'ya say we take off back to my place after this?" she said. "Jason and Ben are involved in a softball tournament all afternoon, and I don't know about you, but for me, watching guys play softball is about as exciting as watching paint dry. Besides, we'll expire in this heat—there's no covered grandstand."

Annabelle gratefully agreed, and half an hour later she followed Daisy's yellow Volkswagen up a rutted driveway and parked her car in front of a ramshackle white cottage.

Annabelle caught a glimpse of Ben's trailer, half a mile away, almost obscured by the surrounding orchards. He and Jason were going to come to Daisy's house when the ball game was over, and he'd promised to bring pizza and ice cream for everyone for dinner.

"Wanna see the joint?" Daisy led the way inside. "When you haven't got money for a decorator," she drawled, "you gotta use your imagination."

The front door led into a short hallway with a large living room off to the right. The walls were painted creamy white, and all down the hall Daisy had stenciled huge, dramatic yellow sunflowers. The living room had only one rather small window that looked out on the orchard, but on the side wall, brown wood-tone paint had been used to mimic a six-foot window-frame with a sunny view of lake, mountain and sky painted inside it. The artistry was amateurish, but the effect delighted Annabelle. It was unique and entertaining and whimsical.

"Jase did the lake scene. The kid's no Rembrandt, but he's not bad, huh?"

The floor was carpeted in twelve-inch squares of different colors and textures that formed a patchwork-quilt design, making the entire room glow with vibrant color.

"I dated a guy who worked for a carpet factory. He gave me all the samples and we glued 'em down. The floor was wrecked anyhow. He was a jerk, but at least the carpet part worked out great."

Two small bedrooms with brightly covered futons placed directly on the floor were on the opposite side of the hall.

"No back problems, sleeping right on the floor," Daisy said philosophically.

Throughout, bright paint and much imagination had created an effect much like Daisy's own personality: vivacious, cheerful and unorthodox.

"I'll get us some iced tea, and we'll go out back and cool off in the pool."

The "pool" turned out to be a child's plastic wader, and Daisy giggled at her own joke. The women dabbled their feet in the cool water, drank gallons of ice tea, and talked about summer dresses, men, makeup, men, real estate and men.

Annabelle's pager summoned her twice, and both times she diplomatically but firmly refused to show properties that afternoon. She was mildly shocked at herself for ignoring business opportunities, but there was always tomorrow. She'd work hard on Sunday, she promised herself. Today, she was visiting with a new friend, and tonight, she was going dancing with Ben, and nothing was going to interfere.

"Hey, I've got this great new polish, it's called Zap 'Em Dead Red," Daisy announced when Annabelle returned from a phone call. "Let's paint our toenails."

MAYBE IT WAS THAT dramatic touch of color peeping out of her open-toed high-heeled sandals that made her feel irresistible, Annabelle reflected as she floated in Ben's arms much later that evening. Or maybe it was the way Ben had looked at her earlier when she came out of Daisy's bedroom wearing the simple, short white dress she'd brought along for the dance.

The dress she'd *bought* for the dance, she corrected herself. She'd seen it in a shop window and had bought it on impulse last Thursday. It bared her arms and neck and more of her thighs than she'd thought decent at first, but the short, swirly skirt was marvelous for dancing, just as the salesclerk had promised.

Something was having a magical effect, that was certain.

"You're the most beautiful woman in the room, Bella," Ben murmured in her ear as he whirled her confidently around to the strains of a waltz. "Every single man here wishes he were in my boots." Ben's strong arms tightened around her and he pressed a lingering kiss just below her ear, stirring wild responses in her midsection.

"They obviously don't know how often I've trampled on your boots." All the same, Annabelle felt herself flush with delight at his ridiculous flattery.

The fact was, the room had its share of beautiful women, but Ben seemed unaware of anyone but her. He looked devastatingly handsome in well-tailored Western pants and a short-sleeve shirt almost the same shade of blue as his eyes. Each time those eyes met hers, they kindled a spark inside her, and his strong arms encircling her made her feel cherished and fragile.

His embrace brought back vivid recollections of their lovemaking, and she felt disappointed because she knew she wouldn't end up in his bed tonight when the dance was over. She was going to have to drive herself back to Kelowna in another couple of hours, and Ben was obligated to stay here at the hall until everyone left—which, he'd told her, would probably be at least dawn.

The band called an intermission when the waltz ended.

"Want to stroll outside and get some fresh air?" The room was getting more crowded all the time, and the air was both sultry and smoky.

Ben held her hand firmly as he threaded his way through the crowd, responding to greetings and good-naturedly fending off innumerable invitations to sit down and have a drink. Annabelle had noticed how popular he was, with women as well as men. She'd been the focus of more than one envious feminine glance during the evening.

Outside, it was balmy, but cooler than inside the hall. There was a breeze off the water. The moon had risen, a huge golden orb in a star-studded sky.

Ben led the way through the crammed parking lot and down a hill to the beach. There was a makeshift bench carved from a log, and he carefully dusted off the seat for her with a tissue. Then he sat beside her and fitted her into the curve of his arm, letting her head rest comfortably on his shoulder. He smelled good—a clean, tangy male odor that she found tremendously appealing.

"Comfortable, Bella?" His voice was a deep, familiar rumble.

"Wonderfully. Ben, I'm so glad I came today. I've had the best time. My stomach still hurts from laughing so much at dinnertime."

Daisy had entertained them with hilarious stories of her childhood on a farm with twin sisters, a madcap mother, and a father trying valiantly to bring Teutonic order to a feminine household patently out of his control. Annabelle was sure Daisy must have been making most of it up, but Daisy insisted every word was true.

Music and voices drifted down from the hall, but the beach was deserted. The moon was reflected on the pewter surface of the lake.

"It reminds me of Greece, this place," she said dreamily. "The warm air, the huge moon, the dark water, the sound of music and laughter."

It surprised her, how painless it was to remember Greece now. For so many years, those memories had been unbearable. When had they changed? When had they become something she could bear to tell Ben?

"That's where you met the man you married." Ben's voice was easy, conversational, but inside, he was alert and tense. She'd never once talked about Theodore Winslow in any sort of detail. She hadn't even mentioned him by name, but Amos had a friend in real estate who'd volunteered that Winslow was Annabelle's ex-husband.

It was common knowledge among the real-estate community that the two were arch enemies.

A little ashamed of himself, but needing to know whatever he could learn about her, Ben had unearthed quite a store of information about Winslow in the past few days. None of it had impressed him. Some of it was downright shoddy.

Annabelle moved her head against his shoulder in assent. "Theodore Winslow. He was an adventurer, a Canadian with a salvage boat who made his money diving for treasure." She gave a sad laugh that tugged at Ben's heart, and he reached over and took her hand in his. "I realize now that he saw right through the romantic twenty-year-old girl I was then. He sensed, of course, that my family had money. He courted me, and I fell insanely in love. I married him a week after we met, over my parents' horrified objections."

She was quiet for a moment, and Ben waited, hoping she'd go on. He wanted to know in detail what

Winslow had done to her that could produce such pain
in her voice after all those years.

"You see, he didn't tell me that he'd made the find of
his life just before I appeared on the scene—a sunken
Greek galleon loaded with artifacts and ancient coins.
Instead of reporting it to the Greek government, he se-
cretly shipped some of the most valuable items out of
the country. He was under investigation when I met
him, and several days after our marriage, the police
came and took him to jail. I was devastated. Fool that
I was, I used a trust fund left me by my grandmother to
buy his freedom." She sighed softly against his shoulder. "Theo was banking on me doing exactly that, of
course. Using my inheritance that way estranged me
from my parents. My father was horrified and re-
volted by what he labeled—" her voice lowered and
became very British in an attempt at humor that tore
at Ben's heart "—an irresponsible alliance with a calculating fortune hunter." She shook her head. "How
right he was. How stupid I was. Anyway, we left Greece
in disgrace and sailed for Canada. Theo had grown up
near here, and he saw the potential for making money
on real estate in the Okanagan."

"Is that when you began selling, too?" Ben had to
conceal the anger toward Winslow that had welled inside him while she talked.

"No. I hardly had time to unpack and arrange the
apartment before he walked out on me." She was being totally matter-of-fact, but Ben could imagine only
too well the agony she must have suffered.

"I was..." She swallowed before she could go on, and
he tightened his grip on her fingers, wordlessly trying
to communicate support.

"I was rather upset, to say the least. He'd met the daughter of a local real-estate tycoon, and Theo was always one to recognize opportunity. He divorced me and married her—it turned out she was pregnant by that time. He eventually inherited the largest real-estate business in the valley. He has three children now." She sounded so forlorn, Ben wanted nothing more than an opportunity to murder Winslow. "Her pregnancy was the hardest thing of all for me. I'd wanted a baby very badly."

Ben swallowed hard before he could manage the next question. "Why did you stay in Canada? I'd have thought going back to England would have been far easier for you than staying here."

"God, how I wanted to." Even now, there was naked longing in her voice. "I didn't know anyone here. I had no job and very little money left. I was an emotional wreck. It was pride that kept me here." She straightened and he loosened his hold on her shoulder, feeling her body tense with remembered emotion. "Pride. Anger. Vindictiveness. I wanted to get back at Theo, you see. I wanted to beat him at his own game."

"So you studied real estate."

"Yes." Her russet hair stirred and fell back into place as she nodded. "I met Cyril Lisk, and he helped me a great deal in the beginning."

"And is revenge worth it, Bella?" He was taking big chances here. "You've given up a lot just to pay Winslow back. You could have remarried, had babies of your own by now."

She was quiet and still for so long he thought he'd blown everything. She turned, finally, and looked into his eyes. He couldn't tell for sure, but he thought the moonlight glinted on tears.

"I never questioned any of it before, Ben. Not until . . ." She looked away and swallowed hard.

"Until what, Bella?" The tension in his body was making his muscles ache.

"Until . . . recently." Her voice was so low he could barely hear her. "Until very recently."

They weren't as much as he'd hoped for, but her whispered words were a beginning. A promise.

He wrapped his arms around her and kissed her.

# 9

AFTER THAT EVENING, Ben took to appearing at her office late in the afternoon when Annabelle was ready to quit for the day.

The first night, he took her to a restaurant nearby for a sumptuous Chinese feast in air-conditioned comfort.

Another evening, they walked along the beach and ate hot dogs and fries from a vendor. They took off their shoes and splashed their feet in the lake to get cool, which somehow ended in a water fight that left both of them drenched and breathless from laughter.

And when it grew late, he left her at the door of her apartment with nothing more than a few passionate kisses and a cheerful good-night—tactics that were making her crazy, as one week followed another.

What was wrong with him?

What was wrong with *her*?

Annabelle tossed and turned and fumed.

Didn't he want to make love to her again? She replayed their lovemaking on Paradise like an X-rated video in her mind, wondering whether she'd been so out of practice that she'd bored him. It hadn't felt like he was bored at the time, but then she'd been enjoying herself instead of analyzing the whole performance.

All in all, her experience was pretty limited, and in recent years nonexistent. Maybe things had changed drastically since she'd last been with a man.

Or could it be that he was waiting for her to make the second move?

She finally turned to an expert for information.

She and Daisy were in Annabelle's car one morning, driving back to the office after viewing a piece of property the owner wanted Midas to sell for him.

Annabelle went over openings in her mind, but Daisy made it easy.

"Johnny's *finally, finally,* asked me for a date," she commented with a huge sigh, popping a fat cherry into her mouth.

Her lips were already stained a deep purple. Cherries were in season in the orchards, and she'd brought a shopping bag of them in to the office for everyone to gorge on.

"He likes me, and he's hot for my body, I know that for sure, but man, he's mighty slow about getting on with it. I thought I was going to have to break down and ask him."

Annabelle was stunned. To the best of her knowledge, Johnny wasn't the least bit slow around women. Quite the contrary, in fact. She'd heard him herself, making dates on the phone with all the aplomb of a practiced womanizer. She'd assumed he'd made his move on Daisy fifteen minutes after meeting her, but apparently it hadn't worked that way.

"Do you... Is that something you do? Ask a man out if he appeals to you?"

Daisy munched another cherry and popped the pit into a small bag she'd brought along for that purpose. "I never have yet. Never had to. Things are supposed to be equal and all that, these days. Women have a perfect right to ask a guy out if they want, but I've found most men still like to be the ones who make the moves."

She giggled. "I let them chase me till I catch them. Know what I mean?"

Annabelle wasn't sure she did. "You mean, you...subtly encourage them, but let them take their sweet time about things?"

Daisy nodded. "Right on. See, I figure men are way more romantic than women when it comes right down to it. Sure, you've got your wham-bang-thank-you-ma'am types, but the real men, the ones you want to spend your life with, they're different." Daisy screwed her face up with the effort of putting what she felt into words. "I think they enjoy the whole courtship thing. They want to feel that they're winning us the way knights did in olden times, fighting battles for their ladies and all that sweet, romantic stuff. Heck, half the time most women have the kids named, the cutlery chosen, and the wedding planned while the man they've got the hots for is still thinking about asking if they might want to have a coffee sometime, right?"

"But what if we don't want marriage? What if all we want is...is...?" What exactly was it she wanted from Ben? She frowned and stepped harder on the gas. It was a problem that she'd never quite managed to think through.

"If all we want is something along the lines of wham, bang, thank you ma'am, you mean?" Daisy went on eating cherries, but she had a thoughtful look on her face. "Times I figured all I wanted was a quickie affair, I found out soon enough I was fooling myself. See, I'm not good at commitment. It scares the hell out of me and I've never been able to sustain a relationship for long. So when I have real feelings for somebody, I won't let myself even think 'forever.' I kid myself into believing all I want is good sex and a fast exit, but it's a big fat lie. Then I set out to wreck whatever it is between us that's special, because I know it isn't going to work anyhow." Her laugh was brittle and sad. "Not *very* stupid, huh?"

"At least you understand what you're doing and why." Daisy's insight impressed Annabelle. She wondered with an uncomfortable feeling in her stomach just how clear her own view of herself and her motives really were. As far as Ben was concerned, they were about as clear as thick fog.

"*Now* I understand, yeah. But my last few affairs have been nothing short of suicidal, and Ben was the one who told me I'd better go see a counselor and figure out what the hell was going on with my head. I mean, there's Jase to consider as well as me. The poor kid has to put up with whoever I'm dating, right? So I went to my doctor, and she sent me to this great woman, Ellen's her name. If you ever need to talk to somebody, I'll give you her number."

Annabelle filed the information for future use. The way her life was going, it might not be long at all before she needed Ellen. She reached across and touched Daisy's hand. "Thanks for being so open and honest with me. It . . . it helps to talk things over."

Daisy snorted. "Seems to me I do most of the talking. You're not a great one for baring your soul, are you?" It was said with such matter-of-fact acceptance, Annabelle couldn't take offense.

Besides, it was the truth.

"It's just that I've never really had a close woman friend to talk to, Daisy. I guess it's something that takes practice."

"Well, I can listen as well as yap, y'know. Practice away anytime."

Annabelle turned into the parking lot behind Midas Realty and turned the engine off. "It's almost lunchtime. I need some new shorts and there's a sale on at the mall. Want to come shopping?"

Daisy's eyes sparkled. "Does this mean we're bosom buddies, or just that you're desperate for shorts?"

Annabelle laughed. "Both, you screwball." She turned the key and started the motor again. "We'd better get out of here fast, or Johnny'll dream up some excuse to come along."

Daisy shot her a knowing look. "Or Ben'll turn up and you'll dump me and climb on the back of his bike. Hey, we've got an hour. What d'ya say we get our eyelashes dyed while we're at it? I know this place that does them for half price."

Annabelle had never considered having her eyelashes dyed. She felt giddy and young and daring as she pulled into traffic. For the moment, at least, Ben and real estate and money problems faded into the background.

It felt good to have Daisy as a friend.

HER EUPHORIA WAS short-lived, however.

She returned to the office just after one, eyelashes dramatically dark, and found an urgent message waiting for her to call Nigel Forbes.

Her stomach twisted as she dialed.

They exchanged the usual polite pleasantries, and then Nigel's voice took on a somber tone. "After our last luncheon, I reviewed your business files, Annabelle."

Her fingers clenched around the receiver and she felt perspiration pop out under her arms.

Nigel's voice droned on, and her heart began to hammer as she translated his proper business language into practical terms.

"I want you to understand, Annabelle, that we're not recalling your loans or canceling your overdraft—nothing that drastic—but unfortunately there will be no extension of your existing loans or overdraft at this time. Of course, we'll be reviewing the file regularly, and this situation could change at any moment."

As the message began to make sense to her, she struggled to keep her voice steady. "Hold it a minute. What you're saying is that you're putting a stop on my line of credit, isn't that right, Nigel?"

He cleared his throat several times. "Regrettably, yes. You could say that. Yes, indeed."

"Nigel." She took a deep, shaky, breath, feeling as if the room were tilting. "Nigel, I'm sure you understand how serious this is for the business. I don't have to tell you that we need working capital to keep us going on a day-to-day basis. I'm afraid I don't understand at all why you're . . . doing this." Her voice broke, and she gulped audibly, cursing herself for losing her composure, pitifully grateful that this whole conversation was taking place on the phone rather than in person, so Nigel at least couldn't see the effect it was having on her.

There were several long beats of silence before he responded.

"Annabelle, because of our . . . friendship . . . I'm going to be candid with you." He cleared his throat again and then said in a ponderous tone, "From what I've seen in the last few weeks, it's evident that there has to be more accountability in your system."

She waited for more, and when it became apparent that was all he was going to say, she stammered out, "Accountability? In our system?"

The words might have been in a foreign language, for all she understood them. She hadn't the faintest idea what Nigel Forbes was talking about, but she did understand that arguing with him would accomplish nothing.

"You realize that I'm going to have to review our options and do whatever I consider best for the business." She was proud of herself for dredging up such brave, defiant words, but Nigel must realize, just as she did, that another bank was less than likely to take her on at this point.

"Of course." He paused again, and then blurted out, "I do hope this won't affect our, umm, relationship, Annabelle."

She had a sudden urge to laugh hysterically and give him the number of Daisy's counselor.

If Nigel considered what they had together a relationship, he needed Ellen much worse than she did.

She hung up the phone, put her head down on the desk, and burst into tears. She desperately wanted to talk to Cy, but he was out for the afternoon and hadn't left a number with the receptionist. Johnny wasn't available, either; he'd gone to a meeting of the Real Estate Board. Daisy had left right after their shopping trip to take Jason to the dentist, so except for Hilda and herself, the office was deserted just when she most needed support.

Feeling sick to her stomach, Annabelle lingered late at her desk, hoping against hope that this would be one of the days Ben made an appearance, but by five forty-five, she decided he wasn't coming, either. She turned off her computer, locked up and went home to her empty apartment, feeling destitute.

She made herself a sandwich, but she couldn't eat it.

She tried to call Cy at home but he wasn't there, and Madeline was even snippier than usual.

*Bitch.* Annabelle slammed down the phone and thought of dialing Ben's number, but the phone was probably unplugged—as usual.

She tried anyway, and the ringing went on and on in her ear.

She had to do something, something physical, or she'd scream. She put on her old black bathing suit and went out to the pool, stroking ferociously from end to end while Nigel's words kept ringing in her head like a tolling bell.

*More accountability.*

*No extension of existing loans.*

She'd lost track of how many laps she'd done when a masculine hand reached down and grabbed her ankle as she turned at the far end of the pool.

Ben knelt above her on the wet concrete, and through a chlorine blur she could see his wonderful smile, his blue eyes looking down at her. She'd never been so glad to see anyone in her entire life.

"You coming out, or should I join you in there?"

"Do you have a suit?" There was no logical reason why having him here should make her feel better, but it did. The anxiety inside her seemed to ease a little.

"No suit." He shook his head, a roguish twinkle in his eyes. "I'm wearing clean undershorts, though. Or I could just jump in nude."

"Most of my neighbors are elderly women. There'd be a mob scene out here in no time—they hardly ever get to see naked men. I'd better come out."

He reached a hand down to her and she grasped it, and he easily hoisted her out of the pool. Then he wrapped her in the towel she'd laid on a nearby chaise longue and rubbed some of the water from her arms and shoulders and hair. He used a thumb to wipe drops from her eyelashes, his touch feather light.

Without even knowing she was upset, he comforted her.

"I thought maybe you'd come out to the trailer with me tonight. Clara looks as though she's getting ready to have her baby and I don't like to leave her alone too long. I can fix you a burger, maybe even a salad."

She didn't even hesitate. "Let me put some clothes on and dry my hair." Maybe being with Ben would dissolve the lead that felt as though it was lodged at the pit of her stomach.

Ben was on his motorcycle, and she decided she'd follow him in her car. "That way, you don't have to leave Clara alone to drive me home," she insisted when he argued.

*That way, I can be the one to leave you at the door with nothing more than a good-night kiss, Ben Baxter.*

When they arrived at Ben's trailer, he went immediately to check on Clara, who was grazing peacefully in the small pen he'd fenced off for her. The three-hundred-pound animal came trotting over to Ben, her banana-shaped ears tilted forward as if she was waiting for him to say something nice to her.

Annabelle followed along, standing safely outside the fence while Ben murmured to the llama.

"I didn't think Cupid would be much of a midwife when the baby came, so I isolated Clara in this small pen," he explained, locking the gate carefully behind him. "Usually if there's other female llamas around at a birthing, they act like aunties and fuss over the mother and baby. They're social animals, and don't need privacy for birthing, but it's always safer not to have the sires in with the dams at such times. Poor old Clara's going to have to do it by herself this time—with Cupid having the vapors in the next pen, undoubtedly."

"Will you have to do anything for her?" Annabelle eyed the rotund animal anxiously. "I'm not exactly an experienced midwife or anything, Ben. In fact, I've never seen anything get born except kittens, and that was years ago when I was a child." She was also still extremely nervous around Ben's menagerie.

He laughed at her and shook his head. "You won't even have to boil water. From what I've been told, llamas have their babies trouble free. I just want to be here, in case she runs into any problems. It's her first. They're called *crías*, llama babies. I can't wait to see this one. I sure hope it's healthy."

"What made you decide to start having llamas as pets anyhow, Ben?" Talking about inconsequential things helped to shove the predicament she was in at the office to the back of her mind.

"I didn't really plan it at all. Some people down the hill were moving to Vancouver, and they had to get rid of Cupid and Clara. So I bought them. I got a bargain—the pair cost me twenty-five thousand." He locked the pen behind him and took Annabelle's hand, leading her over to the deck area.

Annabelle couldn't believe she'd heard him right. She stopped and gaped at him. "Dollars? You spent twenty-five thousand *dollars?* For . . . for *llamas?"*

"Sure. They run more like forty-five now, for a pair."

"But—but they're not good for anything. They're—they're a . . . a totally frivolous animal."

Ben threw back his head and laughed. "You sound exactly like Rico and Amos. To say nothing of Leroy. They damned near had group apoplexy when I bought Cupid and Clara."

It wasn't the first time Annabelle had suspected that Ben's friends, eccentric as they were, still had the right idea about some things. Like marketing his wine, for instance, and buying these llamas.

"Besides," he went on, unperturbed by her reaction, "they're clean, friendly, great for sweaters, excellent pack animals. I had a guy from New Zealand teach me how to shear them early last spring. The wool sells for fifty dollars a pound, although you have to get the guard hairs out of it, which can be a pain. And if Clara's young one's a dam, I could eventually sell her for fifteen or twenty thousand."

Theoretically you could, Annabelle reflected—if anyone else was insane enough to ever want to buy one of these things. She knew only too well that buying was one thing, and selling quite another.

"Actually, I'm considering adding some alpacas to the herd. They're only half the size of a llama, and they have no guard hairs, so all the fibre can be used for weaving. That guy that I talked to at Lake Country Days has twenty alpacas he purchased in New Zealand waiting right now to get out of quarantine. He offered me four—a male and three bred females—for a really good price."

Annabelle was speechless. It seemed the most irresponsible, colossal waste of good money she'd ever heard of.

But it was Ben's money to use any way he wanted, she reminded herself.

"Want a cold beer?" He didn't seem to notice her lack of response at all. He seated her on a comfortable chaise longue. "Or maybe a glass of cold wine?"

"Wine. Please." Annabelle watched him head into the trailer, admiring his lean buttocks encased in the close-fitting blue-jean cutoffs, the easy, athletic swing of his body as he walked.

He was good-looking. He was gentle, intelligent, sensitive, kind. He made her laugh. He listened when she talked. And he was at the same time the most unyielding, impractical, madcap spendthrift of a man she'd ever met.

Alpacas, indeed. Clara had her head stuck through the pole corral, her huge, gentle eyes with their ridiculously long, curling eyelashes fixed on Annabelle.

On impulse, Annabelle got up and walked over to the paddock, gingerly reaching out a hand toward the llama the way she'd seen Ben do. Clara nuzzled her with gentle curiosity, her nose petal-soft and damp. She made a low, humming noise in her throat, a friendly sort of greeting.

Annabelle dared to put her fingers on the llama's neck, feeling the deep softness of her wool. Clara moved toward her, as if she enjoyed the contact and wanted to prolong it.

Annabelle had never had much contact with animals. Stroking the gentle llama with growing confidence, she began to understand the appeal pets had, the wordless comfort of being near a creature that made few demands, yet showed unconditional affection.

"Think you might want one as a pet?" Ben was close behind her, holding out a stemmed glass brimming with wine.

Annabelle accepted it, balancing the full glass carefully as she moved back to her seat on the deck. "A llama?" She shook her head. "My landlord doesn't allow cats, never mind llamas."

"You could always keep her here. I'd take care of her for you." The words were casual, but somehow the air between them became charged. It seemed to Annabelle that he was suggesting much more than caring for a pet.

"I couldn't afford one." She tried for a flippant tone. "Anyway, the bank would seize it as collateral."

Ben gave her a keen look. "You still having problems with the bank, Annabelle?"

Her overwhelming need to talk to someone warred with her pride. It was humiliating to admit that the business was in such dismal financial trouble, especially to a man who casually paid enormous sums for llamas and alpacas. But the burden of silence was overwhelming.

"The bank manager called today. He's decided to shut down our line of credit." Saying it out loud made it even more real. She thought again of what it was going to mean to Midas Realty, and to Pinetree Developments, and a cold shudder rippled through her.

Ben frowned. "That's serious stuff. Did he say why?"

"He said something absolutely asinine about needing more accountability in our system. I don't have the vaguest clue what he's talking about." She gulped her wine and set the glass on the arm of the chaise. "I'll discuss it with my partners tomorrow and we'll see about changing banks," she added with a bravado she was far from feeling. "Anyhow, I don't want to spoil the evening by talking about stupid work problems."

It was true. Now that she'd blurted it all out to Ben, she found herself, perversely enough, not wanting to discuss it further. There really wasn't a thing he could do about her banking problems, for heaven's sake.

"Maybe talking it over would help." He was still looking at her intently, as if he wanted to say more.

"Thanks anyway, but I don't think so, Ben." She slid off the chaise longue and reached down a hand to tug him up beside her. "Besides, I'm getting hungry." It wasn't true, but it was a diversion. "Let's go in. You can make those burgers you promised me, and I'll do the salad."

He hesitated, but only for a moment. He got to his feet, and in one strong, impulsive move pulled her into his arms. He didn't kiss her. Instead, he held her tightly against him, as if he was trying to shelter her.

"Annabelle, love, I need to talk to you...."

His whisper was barely audible. His action was unexpected and she stiffened at first, but then the warmth and delight of being in his arms worked on every nerve ending. She allowed herself to lean against him, to wind her arms around his neck and rest her head on his chest, to soak in his essence and forget everything except the delight of being in his arms. He was strong, solid, and the solace of his embrace brought a measure of peace to the turmoil that had boiled inside her all afternoon. She clung to him, borrowing strength, soaking up security.

Ben moved away first, just a few inches that separated their lower bodies. "No matter how noble my intentions are, sex always has a way of interfering." His voice was thick and uneven, and she could feel the muscles in his arms and back trembling under her fingers. A surge of delight shot through her, pleasure that she could stir him the way he did her.

"That's not such a bad thing, is it?" She knew she was being provocative and brazen as she tipped her head back and looked up into his face. "I want you too, Ben."

This time when he crushed her against him, comfort wasn't a factor in the embrace. His mouth came down, hard and demanding, and his hands cupped her bottom, lifting her, pressing her tight against his groin.

It lit fires within her that had been banked and waiting ever since the day on Paradise. It was what she remembered, what she'd yearned for during long, feverish nights and busy workdays. Her knees grew weak, and she clung to his neck. With lips and teeth and tongue, with hands and body, he ravished, letting her know exactly how much he'd missed her.

Boundless need burst into full bloom inside her, and a wordless plea rose in her throat.

"Hey, Ben?" Jason's strident voice sounded from around the corner of the trailer. "Ben, where are ya?"

"Oh, Lord," Ben groaned.

Annabelle pulled away and tried to compose herself, but Ben's arms were still around her when Jason appeared.

"Ahh, yuck, you guys been kissing." The disgust in the boy's tone was unmistakable. "I guess you want me to take a hike, huh?"

"No such luck, kid." Ben released Annabelle gently, keeping her hand locked in his. "What I want you to do is help me get this barbecue going. You had supper yet?" His voice was ragged.

"Mom got me a milk shake in town, but my face was frozen and I couldn't eat. I had two fillings. It hurt real bad, but it's better now."

"Well, if we get this thing going, there's plenty of burgers and fries to go around. You'll have to call and check with your mom first, though."

"Mom's not home. She had to go to an introductory class on her real-estate course. She couldn't miss it. She said it was okay to come over here for a couple hours, as long as I wasn't bothering you." Jason looked over at Annabelle, and she saw the uncertainty on his sunburned features. He was plainly waiting for her approval before he accepted Ben's invitation.

"I just hope you men are good cooks," she managed to say, smiling at Jason. "I'm going to enjoy sitting around and watching you both work."

"All right. I'll go get the stuff from the shed, right, Ben?"

"Right, tiger." Annabelle admired the effort it must have cost Ben to be so warm and welcoming to Jason, because she knew how let-down and disappointed *she* felt. She also knew beyond a doubt that if Jason hadn't appeared, they'd be inside the trailer right now, on Ben's bed. Her body clenched at the image, and she could see her own regret mirrored in Ben's eyes when he gave her a lingering, eloquent look as Jason ran off for the barbecue starter. As soon as the boy was out of sight, Ben hugged her close for a moment, his lips against her ear.

"Thanks for being such a good sport, babe. The kid gets his feelings hurt easy, and I want him to feel like he's welcome here anytime. The good news is he has to be home at nine. Which leaves hours and hours for us to be alone together. Later."

The next several hours were sweet torture. Ben was the soul of propriety in front of the boy, but the looks he shot Annabelle's way rivaled the white-hot coals on the barbecue. Now and then he'd take her hand unobtrusively and stroke his thumb across her palm, sending waves of need rippling through her.

Once he pressed a fierce, hungry kiss against the base of her neck while Jason was in the bathroom, and his hands stroked down her shoulders and then, slowly and tantalizingly, outlined her aching breasts.

"Later," he whispered in a husky voice.

The hands on Annabelle's watch seemed paralyzed, because nine o'clock took forever to arrive.

At last, the hamburgers were eaten and the mess cleared away with only a half hour left before Jason's curfew. Jason teased Ben until he agreed to play a game of catch. They invited Annabelle to join in, but she insisted she preferred to watch.

There was a lovely camaraderie between man and boy, boisterously tossing the ball, leaping in the air to catch it, hollering good-natured insults to each other in the gathering twilight. There was an intimacy about the scene, and Annabelle allowed herself to fantasize for a few moments, imagining that Jason was their son, hers and Ben's, and that they were a family here at dusk in their own orchard.

But then Jason missed a catch and had to chase it far past the llama paddock, and Ben turned to smile at her—a sensual smile so full of promise it made her move restlessly on her lawn chair; and she reflected that if they were long married, with a child Jason's age, her body wouldn't be in this aroused state, impatiently waiting for Ben's loving. Would it?

Maybe the magic would always be there between them, a tiny, hopeful voice whispered.

How she longed to believe it.

Finally Jason said good-night and went peddling furiously down the hill, and at last—at long last—they were alone.

# 10

"NOW, MY BEAUTIFUL Bella."

Ben lifted her hand, and his mouth traced kisses across the palm, between each finger.

A shiver of excitement made Annabelle's breath catch.

His eyes, smoldering blue, looked into hers. "Where exactly were we when the kid arrived?" He drew her into his arms and kissed her, and then pulled back. "I'm all sweaty after that game with Jason. I've got to have a shower. How are you at washing backs, Bella?"

"Pretty rusty," she said, shakily.

He laughed. "Nothing like a little practice, then. C'mon."

His trailer was neat and clean today—not that she was in the least concerned with good-housekeeping points as he drew her through the kitchen and down the hallway to the bathroom at the rear.

Here, too, things were in order. Sink and bathtub gleamed from a recent scrubbing, and there wasn't a sign of red undershorts—not even when Ben unfastened the snap at his waistline and let his cutoffs drop with a thunk to the floor.

Underneath, the scrap of cotton straining to contain him was navy blue.

"Can't get your clothes all wet, can we?" His voice was hoarse and his nimble fingers undid the front closure of her blouse and slid it down her arms.

Her shorts were next. He hooked his thumbs under the waistband and skimmed them down over her hips.

"Bella. My lovely Bella," he crooned, running his hands down her shoulders, making every inch of her skin aware of his nearness, his heat, his touch as he undid the catch at the back of her bra and allowed that, too, to slide down and off her arms.

He drew in a deep, ragged breath and his head bent to suckle at each nipple in turn, making her breath come in short, sharp gasps.

Only her panties were left—provocative scraps of lace, worn, she realized now, with exactly this in mind.

He drew her forward until their mouths and bodies touched, both naked except for the minute barriers of white satin and navy cotton.

She could feel him trembling—tremors that traveled through the muscles her hands caressed as she laid them, palms flat, on his sweat-sheened chest. She found the hair-encircled male nipples, already hard buds, and rubbed a thumbnail across each, relishing the deep, throaty sound that escaped his lips. Shamelessly, she worked his undershorts over his erection and down his hips and thighs until they joined the puddle of clothing on the tile floor.

"Shower, Bella. I need to have a shower," he mumbled against her hungry mouth, his lips greedily devouring hers. He reached out blindly and turned the faucets on, but instead of moving into the spray his hands were on her back, sliding down, laying tracks of fire on her skin. He slid his fingers beneath the elastic of her panties and cupped her bottom, then lifted until her feet were clear of the tile and she was suspended against him, pressed against the straining flesh at the apex of his thighs.

His fingers slid lower, deeper, into her wetness and heat, and instinctively she moved her legs apart to make room for his exploring hand.

It was her turn to cry out when his fingers found her hot, damp flesh.

Impatiently, he stripped her panties off, kneeling in front of her, his mouth following the path his hands traveled, down her belly and thighs.

She made tiny sounds of approval and delight, wanting more.

With a muffled exclamation, he got to his feet, stepped into the shower, and drew her in with him.

The water made her breath catch—it was cool on her overheated body, and the spray played across every sensitive nerve-ending, heightening her arousal.

Ben nibbled at her lips and throat and used the soap carelessly, quickly, on his chest and underarms, between his legs, and then, with much more attention to detail, he rubbed a coating across her breasts and shoulders, down to her belly, across her back.

His work-roughened fingers and palms felt exquisite against her skin. His fingers slipped lower, gliding with tantalizing slowness between her thighs, touching the swollen flesh, expertly soothing and inciting it at the same time.

Arms wrapped around his neck, she moved against him, and he lifted her until her legs locked around his waist and she felt his hard shaft suddenly thrust deep inside her.

Her climax began at that instant of penetration, and she rocked in ecstasy, raising her legs still higher to contain him, to bring her body in even closer contact with his as wave after wave of rapture undulated through her.

Her movements drew a guttural cry from his throat, and his arms tightened around her until she could barely breathe. With driving, pulsating force he thrust up and into her, over and over again, pushing them both back against the wall of the shower. His body shook, and his head was thrown back so that water cascaded across his eyes and nose and mouth.

He trembled, and with eyes tightly shut he slid down the wall and collapsed on the bottom of the shower stall, still holding her against him.

"Ben, we're going to drown," she warned at last, trying to push his hair and her own out of their eyes as the shower gushed relentlessly over them.

He opened one eye and peered at her. "I didn't know drowning felt this good," he whispered hoarsely. But he stretched an arm up and managed to turn the faucet off.

Somehow, they tumbled out, a welter of arms and legs. Ben found a giant-size towel and wrapped her in it, rubbing himself dry and then tenderly drying her, kissing parts of her anatomy as he blotted them free of water.

Finally they collapsed in a heap on his bed, her head nestled against his chest, his arms encircling her. Annabelle snuggled against him, loving the smell of him, the feel of his skin against hers.

"How come you waited so long to make love to me again?" She was totally relaxed, completely at ease, which is why she dared to be so direct. But she wanted to know.

It took him several moments to answer. "I didn't want you to think making love was the only reason I wanted to be with you," he said at last. "You're special to me, Bella. Special here." His hand touched the nest of hair between her thighs in an intimate acknowledgment of their loving. "And here." He moved his fingers up to stroke them through her wet hair, cupping her skull to indicate her mind. He moved his hand down and laid it gently against her breast, where her heart thrummed with exhaustion and contentment. "And most of all, here." There was a long pause, and then he said simply, "I love you, Bella. I've fallen in love with you, and I don't want to do anything to spoil that."

He raised his head and looked into her eyes, and then bent to kiss her with gentle passion; and this time, his lovemaking was slow, tender, giving, devoid until the very end of the savage hunger that had been there both times before. As long as he was able, Ben saw to it that each movement, each response, was richly savored, unhurried. But at last the slow, delicious building within each of them—the holding back—demanded completion, and it came with an echo of the same rich passion they'd enjoyed before.

"I love you, Bella," he said again, and she knew he was waiting for her answer. She tried out the words in her mind, and they sounded right, but caution had become a habit that was hard to break. It kept her silent.

Sweat-sheened, she fell asleep instead, cushioned by his arms, wrapped in the delicious scent of musk the sheets had captured.

She awoke in the dark, feeling anxious, knowing it was late and that he was no longer beside her. The bedside clock read two forty-three.

One of his shirts hung over a chair, and she shoved her arms through the sleeves and fumbled with a couple of buttons. A trip to the bathroom told her that falling asleep with wet hair led to some strange results, and she used his hairbrush to try to straighten out the mess and finally gave it up as a hopeless job.

Still groggy, she stumbled down the hallway in search of him.

There was a soft light on at the front of the trailer, and Ben was sitting in an armchair in the living area, a cup of coffee resting on one jeans-clad knee. His feet and upper body were bare. He looked up and smiled at her as she sank down onto the couch.

She tugged his shirt down over her bare thighs. "I missed you. I woke up and you were gone."

"I couldn't sleep," he confessed. "I made some coffee. Want a cup?"

She shook her head and yawned. What she wanted was to go back to bed with him, to curl against him and fall asleep knowing he'd be there when she awakened, a buffer against the daytime things that threatened to overwhelm her.

She wanted to reach a place where it was easy to voice her love for him. She needed him to help her, to lead her to that place. She was learning to trust, but it was difficult and slow.

"Annabelle," he began.

The formal use of her name surprised her. He always called her Bella, these days.

"I've been doing some investigating, and there's something you have to know about your business partner, Johnny Calvados. I should have told you before, but somehow the right moment never came. Last evening, when you told me what your bank manager said about accountability, it hit me right away. The bank figures somebody's being dishonest. They wouldn't know who or how it was happening, but the accounts must show some discrepancy that makes them suspicious."

Like a tidal wave, all the problems she'd submerged came rushing out from the deep, dark place where she'd hidden them hours earlier. Her fingers clenched into fists, nails cutting into her palms. She was wide-awake now, waiting for things she didn't want to hear, heart banging against her ribs.

"What about Johnny?" Her voice was strained and high, already defensive even before she knew.

"Johnny Calvados was arrested in New Brunswick ten years ago, for fraud. He was using the name Johnny Whiting then, but there's no doubt it's the same man. The charges were dropped, but all the same, I think maybe your money problems at work could be his doing."

"Who told you all this? How do you even know it's true?" The idea that one of her partners could be cheating the business—cheating her—was unbearable. She trusted Cy and Johnny; they were her friends. More than that, the business had been all she had to care about for a long time. If it was built on lies and deceit, what was left for her to trust?

"I don't believe it." She glared at him as if the whole thing was his fault.

"Oh, it's true, all right." His voice was flat, but assured. "I have a contact in the force. He ran a check through CPIC." Ben's voice was quiet and confident.

"CPIC?" She frowned.

"Canadian Police Information Center."

He'd gone to the police, checking up on her friends. The knowledge stunned her. "Why, Ben? Why are you going around checking on my partners?" Annabelle was trembling, and part of her knew she was being defensive and unreasonable, but what he'd done felt like an invasion of privacy. "I didn't ask you to do this. You had no right to go behind my back."

He frowned. "Look, you're having serious money problems. The first thing that comes to my mind is that somebody in the business is being dishonest. It's a logical conclusion. But I couldn't just tell you I was suspicious, with nothing concrete to back up how I felt. I had to have facts."

His calculated reasoning maddened her. He'd treated her confidences like a police matter to be investigated, and he saw nothing wrong with that.

"Facts," she spat out. "How do you know what really happened? Did you even bother to ask Johnny, face-to-face?" She could see by his expression that he hadn't. "I happen to trust my partners. Did you check up on Cyril, too? And what about me? Did you run one of these . . . these . . . CPIC checks on me, as well?"

"Hey, calm down." Ben got up and came over to her, kneeling beside her chair. He put out a hand and touched her arm, but she jerked away. "Don't be mad at me, Bella. I was only trying to help. I know you've been worried about money. I guessed that your businesses are having pretty serious problems."

Part of her, a rational part, warned that none of this was Ben's fault, but she couldn't seem to stop herself. The pressures of the past few months erupted inside her like a volcano and reason was smothered in the flow of anger and the feeling of betrayal that engulfed her.

"Yes, I've been worried. Yes, my businesses are in danger of failing." Her voice was shrill and high, and the part of her that could still reason was appalled, but she couldn't seem to stop.

"Instead of sneaking around and investigating my partners and…and for all I know, me as well, did it ever occur to you that the companies' financial problems would be solved if you'd stop being so pigheaded about Likely Cove? You're the real reason we're in trouble, Ben, not Johnny, and some—some phony fraud charge that happened years ago. I've tried *everything* to make you see reason about that damned cove…." Her voice faltered as Ben's face drained of color.

His eyes narrowed and his mouth tightened.

He got to his feet and faced her, hands low on his hips.

"Is that the reason you're here right now, Annabelle?" He didn't raise his voice, but there was a lethal tone in it that sent a warning shivering down her spine. "Does 'everything' include sleeping with me to get what you want?" She'd never seen his eyes as blue or as cold.

She took defense in rage. "How dare you insinuate—"

He cut her off, his temper taking over. "Cut the crap, Annabelle. The truth is you've been using me to try and get a sale, and I've been too stupid to recognize what was going on. It's the oldest trick in the book—sex for favors."

It wouldn't have hurt as much if she hadn't loved him. She felt as if he'd slapped her, and any shreds of control evaporated in a primitive urge to slap back, to hurt him as deeply as he'd wounded her.

"Don't you dare call me filthy names, Ben Baxter!" she heard herself shrieking hysterically. "At least I'm out there trying, working hard at something I believe in, instead of sitting up here on a mountaintop studying my…my navel and wasting money on…on llamas, or alpacas, or whatever they are. The simple truth is, you can't handle change of any sort. You don't even have enough ambition to . . . to recognize a business opportunity when it walks up and hits you on the nose."

"You may see Likely Cove as a business opportunity. I don't."

"I'm not talking about the cove. I'm talking about your wine."

"Wine?" He sounded as if he'd never heard the word before. "What about my wine?"

"Don't play dumb. Daisy told me you could have made a fortune with your wine, but you couldn't be bothered to even try. You . . . you just don't have any ambition." Seething with rage, she stormed past him, down the hall and into the bedroom. She scrabbled around on the floor, searching for her underwear, but it was nowhere to be found. Finally she tore his shirt off and pulled her crumpled shorts and top on over bare skin.

Thank God she had her own car. Her purse was in the bathroom, and she snatched it up and started down the hallway.

Ben stood there, blocking her way, one bare arm on each wall. With the light behind him, she couldn't see his face, but the tension in his posture and the strain in his voice were evident.

"Annabelle, I don't want it to end like this. Come and sit down, have some coffee. We'll both cool down and talk things over."

Hurt and angry, she steeled herself against him. "There's nothing more to say, Ben. Let me by."

He hesitated briefly and then dropped his arms and stood to the side. She moved past him, careful not to touch him, and hurried to the front door.

"I've done all the running up till now, Annabelle." His voice was as cold and clear as ice water. "That's over. From here on, if you want to see me, you'll have to come to me."

HE HEARD HER STALL the engine twice before the motor caught. As she turned the car around, he heard her spinning her wheels, and he knew right then he was making a mistake, letting her go like this.

He went racing for the door. He reached it, flinging it back just as she powered her way down the drive and through the gate.

"Annabelle!" he roared after her into the early dawn. "Annabelle, get the hell back here!"

But her taillights were disappearing down the twists and turns of Middlebench Road. His voice came echoing back to him, and Susie raced out of her doghouse, barking hysterically.

He swore in a steady stream and went back inside, slamming the door with a violence that made the whole trailer shake. He threw himself down on the couch and tried to figure out how the hell things had ended up in a bloody mess like this, just when they were moving along so well.

He rubbed an exasperated hand across his eyes and tried to think it through, tried to get past the anger he felt.

He'd tried to do her a favor, and she'd thrown it back in his face as if he were the one who'd been charged with fraud, for cripes' sake.

Then she'd said something that had really hurt, that for an insane moment had made him think she was using him, playing with his feelings, just to get Likely Cove.

Now he'd cooled down a little and could think straight about it, he knew it wasn't that way. It couldn't be. She couldn't pretend to have the responses he knew he'd aroused in her. That they'd aroused in each other, he amended as the memory of the night before came rushing back in vivid detail to haunt him.

But she'd never once said she loved him, either. Had she?

He wasn't gut sure enough of her to feel secure, so like an idiot, he'd lost his temper and said things he shouldn't have said, damn his mouth.

He scowled and thought of what had come next—the torrent of angry words she'd unleashed upon him.

She had a temper that almost matched his own. He had to feel admiration for her spunk, standing up to him the way she had. Trouble was, she'd found his weakest spot and stuck a knife in and twisted it.

He'd never admitted to a living soul that he sometimes had his doubts about the way he'd chosen to live his life. Rico and the others razzed him a lot about shirking adult responsibility and hiding out from reality, and he laughed it off and needled them right back about being jealous.

He'd chosen his path, and he intended to pursue it, but that didn't mean there wasn't a nasty little voice inside that suggested maybe they were right; maybe he was being irresponsible, living his life to suit only himself, doing the things he most enjoyed and saying to hell with the establishment.

Bella'd homed right in on those secret misgivings, except she had the wrong slant on the wine thing and she didn't understand the alpaca business at all.

He'd all but forgotten about the wine.

Two years before, as a joke that backfired, Rico had entered Ben's red wine in the Okanagan Wine Festival, and to Rico's chagrin and Ben's amusement, it had won first prize in the amateur division.

One of the local wineries had then approached him. Their offer included wages while he worked with their vintner for a season, a flat and not-very-generous sum for the outright purchase of his recipe, a lot of local notoriety and very little else.

Ben turned the offer down, but some wicked portion of his ego kept him from telling Rico and the others all the details. He'd let them think he was refusing a deal that could have netted him a fortune. Well, dishonesty had now backfired on him in a big way.

He'd have to set Bella straight about it.

He'd have to set her straight about a lot of things.

But the more he thought about what she'd said, the more a sick certainty filled him. Underneath, part of her must really believe he *was* a lazy bum, wasting his time and money on useless pets.

It hurt—more than he'd imagined it could.

Granted, he'd never explained to her about his extensive and very successful investment portfolio; and he hadn't had a chance to tell her about the intensive research he was conducting right now into setting up a textile business in the Okanagan using alpaca wool. It was an idea that he and several other businessmen felt could result in a multibillion-dollar industry over the next ten or twenty years. But it was a gamble, an adventure.

What she didn't know was how well he could afford to speculate. He'd shown her only the part of him he wanted her to see, because that's the part he knew would be hardest for her to accept. Some rebellious demon in him wanted her to love him just the way he appeared to be, an idle wine-making hippie living a hand-to-mouth existence in a battered trailer in an orchard.

Well, it hadn't worked, had it? She wanted something else.

*Someone* else.

Inside, he felt disillusioned and heartsick about the whole affair.

He got up and glanced through the window at the llama paddock. "I'll be damned." He was out the door before he remembered his bare feet, and he had to race back inside to pull on a pair of runners.

Inside the paddock, Clara hovered over her newborn daughter making comforting humming sounds, and gave Ben a triumphant, proud glance when he hurried inside.

"You went and had your baby all by yourself, Clara. Oh, just look at her!" Ben exclaimed.

The long-necked, long-legged *cría* was already tottering around the enclosure, and Cupid was almost strangling himself in an effort to push his head farther through the poles in an effort to greet his daughter.

"C'mere and let me have a look at you, little thing."

The baby llama was adorable. Ben knelt and took the tiny creature in his arms, feeling a rush of tenderness and wonder at her perfection and beauty, her newborn delicacy.

But his pleasure was muted by his overwhelming desire to share this miracle with Annabelle. He'd wanted more than anything to have her by his side at this moment, marveling with him at the softness of the baby's wool, laughing with him at the ridiculous eyelashes that shaded the *cría*'s huge, innocent eyes.

She'd spoiled this moment, taken away some of the joy.

He couldn't help feeling angry and betrayed. And now that anger grew into a stubborn fury, fueled by the loneliness and longing for her he felt at this moment of birth.

He'd stick to what he'd said. She was going to have to take the next step—if there *was* a next step for the two of them.

AUGUST WAS BREAKING ALL records for heat.

Annabelle bought an air conditioner for her bedroom, but even the blessed coolness didn't result in sleep. The nights crawled past while she tossed and turned and finally got up to sit in a desolate stupor in front of the television, watching old movies she couldn't remember a single thing about when morning finally came.

She thought of Ben almost constantly, and she thought of work, but a peculiar numbness seemed to protect her from feeling deeply about either issue. She kept herself under strict control, but she couldn't make herself sleep.

The morning after she drove home from Ben's, she showered, dressed and then marched into the office and told Cy and Johnny what had happened with the bank, leaving out the part about more accountability in the system.

When they left her office, she phoned the accounting firm and asked for a full audit on Pinetree and Midas, with the results to come directly to her. If there was

a shred of truth in what Ben had said about Johnny—
and she'd begun to admit that maybe there was a faint
possibility Ben's information might be correct—then
an audit would be a certain way of exposing it.

Exposing Johnny. The very thought made her ill.

Those first few days after their quarrel, she more than
half expected Ben would come to her, but when eight
days had gone by with no sign of him, she accepted that
their parting was final.

The blessed numbness dissolved, and on the ninth
morning she arrived at work with chalky skin and
blotchy eyes from crying half the night.

She'd admitted to herself, finally, how much she
loved Ben and what his loss meant to her. Pride and fear
kept her from contacting him. She'd been rejected once
by someone she loved, and the memory of that pain
was deep and frightening.

She couldn't afford a second time.

"You look like you could use coffee and a doughnut," Johnny remarked, setting the two items on her
desk and sitting down with his own steaming mug. He
sipped his coffee and shifted nervously in his chair.
"There's something I want to talk to you about, Annabelle."

Annabelle felt nauseous and weak, repelled by the
smell of the coffee, sweaty in spite of the cold shower
she'd had not an hour before.

She looked across at Johnny, handsome and well
dressed but ill at ease; and with a sense of horror, she
knew he was about to admit to her that he was embez-
zling money from the business, that all Ben's accusa-
tions about fraud were well-founded, that she'd been
dead wrong about everything.

Instead, he crossed and uncrossed his long legs, ran a hand through his dark curly hair and then blurted out, "Annabelle, I've asked Daisy to marry me and she's said yes. I wanted you to be the first to know."

# 11

HORROR-STRICKEN, Annabelle gaped at Johnny.

"You . . . and Daisy . . . ?"

Johnny shifted in his chair. "We haven't known each other that long, but neither of us wants to wait. And because of our kids, we don't think it's a good idea to just move in together," Johnny said. He leaned forward, face suffused with emotion. "God, Annabelle, I've never felt this way in my life before—not about Caroline, not about anybody. Daisy's the most beautiful woman I've ever met. I can't believe she feels the same way about me that I do about her."

"Johnny, I . . . I hardly know what to say. I had no idea. I mean, you've only known Daisy a matter of weeks. . . ."

A little less than she'd known Ben, a tiny, sad voice reminded. If things had been different, would her and Johnny's roles be reversed right now?

"I feel as if I've known her always. When something's right, you feel it in your gut, Annabelle."

Annabelle's own gut rumbled alarmingly, and bile rose in her throat.

She'd felt that certainty, that sense of rightness, every single time she was in Ben's arms. She just hadn't had the courage these two had, to express openly how she felt and what she wanted.

"Anyhow," Johnny was saying, "what I wanted to talk over was the business. The deadline's coming up fast on our development parcel out by Likely Cove, and I don't think there's a hope in hell Ben's going to sell to us."

Annabelle nodded, cringing inside when she remembered what she'd said to Ben.

*"I've tried everything...."*

No wonder he'd lost his temper. She tried to pay attention to what Johnny was saying, but she was feeling more nauseous by the minute.

Johnny didn't seem to notice. "Now there's this problem with our cash flow at the bank," he was saying in a worried tone. "The whole thing has me concerned. I mean, I'm going to be taking on a family, and I need to feel financially secure. Is there anything I can do to help us over this bad spot, Annabelle? I mean, besides working my behind off at residential sales—I'm doing that anyway. I really want to help the company over this, any way I can." Annabelle felt like a balloon deflating. She couldn't sit and look into Johnny's earnest brown eyes and believe for one moment he was an embezzler.

And yet . . . Ben had been so certain.

Her stomach rebelled.

"Johnny, I'm not feeling well this morning. Could we talk about this again another time?" Without waiting for an answer, she bolted for the bathroom and was miserably ill.

She felt responsible for ever introducing Daisy to Johnny. She felt as though her whole world was collapsing around her ears.

*Arrested for fraud, using another name*, Ben had stated about the man with whom Daisy had apparently fallen head over heels in love.

Annabelle splashed cold water on her face and wished with all her heart she hadn't been as harsh with Ben as she had. He might be able to figure out what should be done about all this.

Harsh, hell. She'd been downright nasty. And it wasn't for Daisy's sake she wanted Ben; it was for her own.

*You followed your heart once and lived to regret it. Ben's irresponsible. It would never work; you know that.*

She slumped against the wall. The results of the audit would be coming in later in the week. When they did, and if they showed that Johnny was indeed defrauding the business, she was honor-bound to tell Daisy the truth.

And break her friend's heart.

The same way her own was breaking?

BEN'S TEMPER disintegrated as day after day went by with no word from Annabelle. He'd even plugged the damned phone in and left it plugged, but it just sat there on the counter, silent and taunting.

After a few mishaps, his friends gave him a wide berth. Jason should have made himself scarce as well, but it seemed as if the kid was underfoot twenty-six hours a day, just when Ben would prefer to be alone.

Today Jase was doing every single stupid thing boys did when they were determined to be annoying.

"Jase, I told you to turn that damn radio down. I can't hear myself think." Ben scowled at the boy, sweat dripping off his forehead, and with a mutinous glare, Jason turned the dial down an infinitesimal amount.

"Jeez, Ben, it's Hammer. It's rap, it's gotta be loud. Where you been livin'?"

"Turn it down, and keep it down, or I'll turn it off."

"How come we never do anything fun anymore? You said we could go fishing one day. The summer's nearly over."

The boy's whine grated on Ben's nerves. "I told you, I've got work to do." Ben had decided that morning that the best cure for insomnia was physical exhaustion, so he'd started enlarging the llama paddock for the eventual arrival of the alpacas he'd bought.

Jason was supposed to help carry poles up from the pile by the garage. He'd managed two in forty minutes, complaining steadily about the heat, needing a drink, having to use the bathroom, and, under his breath, making remarks about Ben being a slave driver.

The boy was generally being a pain in the butt, and what little patience Ben had was fast disappearing.

"Go get another couple poles for me." Ben shoveled out the last of a posthole. The sun felt as if it was shrinking his skull.

Jason wandered at a snail's pace over to the stack and instead of bringing a pole, he began chucking rocks dangerously close to the trailer. Susie chased after them, certain that this was a game, barking at the top of her lungs. The llamas grew restless and milled around their pen, humming anxiously over the baby.

"Jason, you're gonna hit something. Now cut it out, would you?"

The words were hardly out of Ben's mouth when there was a crash. The large window on the side of the trailer now had a sizable hole, and shards of glass were scattered over the grass.

"Jason, get the hell over here. Right now!" Ben's furious roar silenced the dog. Tail between her legs, she ran for her kennel, and the boy came slouching across the yard, head down, face resentful.

Ben took two long strides toward him, grasped him by the shoulders and gave him a hard shake, and then another. "Damn it all, what the hell's wrong with your brains," he shouted, "throwing rocks at the trailer? Don't you have better sense than to do a thing like that?"

Jason's sunburned face crumpled. He twisted violently out of Ben's grasp, tears pouring down his cheeks, and ran for his bike, propped against the corner of the toolshed.

For a moment, Ben's inclination was to let him go, and good riddance. Then, the image of the boy's unhappy face registered, and he sprinted across the yard and grabbed the back of the bike.

"Hold it, Jase. I didn't mean to yell at you like that. It's only a damned window. We can easily fix it."

"I didn't mean...mean to..." Jason was sobbing too hard to talk, rubbing filthy hands across his tear-stained face, head bent in shame.

"I know you didn't, partner. Lets go inside and get a cool drink. It's too bloody hot to be out here, anyhow." Ben looped an arm across the boy's thin shoulders and they dodged around the glass on the doorstep.

Inside, Ben handed Jason a cola and popped the tab from a can of cold beer for himself, watching unobtrusively as the boy struggled to gain control of himself.

"I'll pay for the window glass, Ben. I got some allowance saved."

"You can work it off." Ben tipped the icy can to his lips and let the cool liquid wash down his throat. "We've gotta get that pen done before the alpacas get out of quarantine. That could be any day now."

Jason also downed half his cola in one long draught. "There's something I need to ask you, Ben."

Ben studied the somber expression on the boy's face. It dawned on him that something was bothering the kid—something besides the window—and he'd been too wrapped up in his own problems the last week or so to even notice. "So ask away."

"When my mom gets married, can I come and live with you? Please, Ben, I'll work like hell for you, I promise. I won't be no trouble."

Ben frowned and shoved the dirty dishes far enough back so he could set his can on the table. "What makes you think your mom is even thinking of getting married?" Daisy always had some guy or other around, but this was the first he'd heard of anybody serious.

"Because they told me they were going to. Her and that Johnny." Jason's voice was filled with disdain. "He's already got a kid, a *girl*. He brought her over— she's a nerd. And she'll probably even have to come and live with us."

"Your mom and Johnny?" Ben didn't try to hide his astonishment. "Not Johnny Calvados? The real-estate guy?"

Jason nodded. "Yeah. He's around all the time now. And Mom had this talk with me, like what would I think if she got married, and did I like Johnny, and crap like that."

Ben was horrified. He carefully hid his reaction from the boy. "Did your mom say how soon this was going to happen?"

Jason shook his head. "But you know Mom—she sorta rushes into things a lot."

That was the understatement of the century, Ben concluded.

The last thing Jason needed was a criminal for a stepfather.

Before Annabelle had walked out on him, Ben had planned to offer his help at finding out a lot more about Johnny Calvados and whether or not he was defrauding Midas Realty and Pinetree Developments.

He'd tossed that idea out along with all his dreams of a future for himself and Bella. He'd done a lot of thinking the past week, and the more he thought about it, the less he figured it would ever work, him and Annabelle.

The bottom line must be that she wanted a different sort of guy, or she'd have called by now.

It looked as if he'd best go ahead with the investigation anyway. Better Daisy find out that she was mixed up with a crook before she jumped headfirst into marriage—not that a criminal record would necessarily stop her. Daisy's mind worked in mysterious ways.

"Maybe we ought to pack up some lunch and go fishing this afternoon, Jase," Ben said thoughtfully. "It looks like I'm gonna have to do some business in town the next few days, and we might not get another chance before school goes back, because I'm expecting a call any day about the alpacas. I'll have to go and pick them up when they're released from quarantine. So today's the day to catch a whopper. What d'ya say?"

Jason's smile spread across his freckled face like liquid sunshine.

Fishing rod in hand, Ben mapped out in his mind that afternoon the various ways someone could have defrauded Pinetree Developments. The next morning he began calling tradespeople who might have bidden on jobs for the company.

Rico turned out to have a contractor friend who was a big help, giving Ben the names of surveyors, excavating companies, underground services, men who did paving, concrete workers.

Then came the tedious job of tracking individuals down and asking questions.

It took nearly a week, but he gradually learned what he needed to know.

It seemed the same companies got all the work for Pinetree on every property they developed. Figuring that policy must cause hard feelings, Ben sought out a few of the businesses that didn't work for Pinetree, especially the ones who weren't doing so well right now.

Finally, he hit pay dirt.

The man's name was Nickleson, and he had an excavating business on the verge of bankruptcy. He'd bidden on jobs for Pinetree, without any success, even though his bids were ridiculously low.

"All I wanted was to keep my men working, keep the crew together. I know for a fact nobody could have bidden any lower, but I didn't get the jobs." He squinted at Ben through a haze of cigar smoke. "So I asked around. Seems like almost everybody in the trades knows what's going on. It's no big secret. Kickbacks, that's the name of the game with those shysters. Anything from a couple hundred to a few grand on every contract, depending on how big the job is. Honest Joes like me won't go for this under-the-table stuff, so guess who's working right now and who isn't. Makes me wonder sometimes whether it's worth it, being straight."

"Who okays the bids? Who's getting the money at Pinetree?" Ben knew beyond a doubt what Nickleson would say. *Once a crook, always a crook, huh, Johnny boy?*

Nickleson shook his head. "I don't know his name. I saw him a couple times. One of the guys working for me used to work for one of the companies Pinetree does business with—he pointed him out. White-haired guy, real bushy eyebrows, drives a big black Caddy with Midas Realty stamped on the door."

Cyril Lisk. Shock waves rippled through Ben. "More than one guy in on it, you figure?"

"Not that I ever heard."

For the rest of that day and most of the next, Ben conducted a quiet and thorough investigation of Cyril Lisk, calling in favors from various friends and members in the RCMP. What he found out backed up what Nickleson had said.

Lisk lived in a lakeside mansion valued at one million. His wife drove a Porsche sports car. They spent a month each winter in Hawaii, where it seemed Lisk owned not just a condominium apartment, but an entire building. No doubt about it, his private assets and general standard of living appeared to far exceed his declared annual income.

Ben, still suspicious, then turned his attention to Johnny Calvados.

Johnny lived in a moderately priced apartment in town. He drove an old Mustang convertible and seemed to lead a frugal existence, giving a large portion of his income to his ex-wife for alimony and child support. There was no indication whatsoever that he had more to his name than the two thousand two hundred dollars presently in his savings account.

Remembering what Annabelle had said, Ben decided to ask Johnny point-blank about the fraud charges. He followed the realtor home, watched him go inside his apartment and then knocked on the door.

"Hi, Ben." Surprise registered on Johnny's face, but he was polite and welcoming. "C'mon in."

The apartment was sparsely furnished, cheap, functional, bargain basement. Ben noted that Johnny had made a real effort to make the place homelike; there were healthy-looking plants here and there, and his daughter's paintings were carefully framed and hung on the living-room walls. There were school pictures of her on the coffee table.

"Sit down. Care for a beer? There're a couple of cold ones in the fridge."

"I'll pass on the beer." It wasn't Ben's style to drink a man's beer at the same time he was interrogating him. "I wanted to ask you a couple of questions, and I need some straight answers."

Johnny gave him a long look and then nodded. He took a chair across from Ben and waited, meeting Ben's eyes with a steady glance.

"I've been doing some digging," Ben began, holding the other man's gaze. "Seems you had a few problems about ten years ago, back in New Brunswick." Ben outlined what he knew about the fraud charges and then waited for the other man's reaction.

Johnny looked shocked. He shook his head and blew out a long breath. "You've got me off guard. I figured you were here because you'd heard about me and Daisy, and you wanted to talk about Jason. I know how close you are to the boy."

"Wouldn't you say this concerns Jason?"

"Yeah, I figure it does. Which is why I told Daisy about that fraud charge, weeks ago when we started getting serious."

Ben concealed his surprise. "I didn't get my information from her, in case you're wondering."

Johnny gave Ben a level look. "I wasn't. I know Daisy."

It was said with such confidence, such loving certainty, that Ben felt respect and a tinge of envy for the other man.

Johnny sighed. "About the fraud charge. It was a long time ago. I was a cocky, ambitious kid with a chip on my shoulder and not much education. My father was a hard man. He kicked me out when we didn't see eye-to-eye about me staying on the farm. I was down on my luck, and I met this businessman, Greenberg. He hired me to sell home renovations, new roofs, upgraded wiring, things like that. Turned out I was a born salesman." Johnny smiled with grim humor. "Trouble was, it was all a con. The work got done, all right, but it wasn't done properly. Took a while for people to catch on. By that time, we'd moved on to new territory." He shook his head. "My conscience finally kicked in—long overdue, I grant you. A couple of the people I sold to were old, not much money. I started having trouble sleeping at night. So I went to the cops. They dropped the charges against me in return for giving evidence against Greenberg."

He stood and walked over to pick up a picture of his daughter. "I learned a hard lesson, and I've never forgotten it. I've been bone honest ever since. I don't have the stomach for a life of crime."

"How come you were using an alias?" Ben needed all the blanks filled in.

Johnny laughed, this time with real humor. "Typical teenage-rebellion thing. I was hurt and pissed off at my old man when I left home, so I decided to use Whiting, my mother's maiden name, instead of his. I figured that would really fix him good. What it did was keep his name off the police records."

"There's one other thing I don't understand. There was a sizable check from a sale you made at Midas that went missing a few weeks ago."

Johnny frowned. "I don't understand what happened with that check myself. I've gone over it in my head. I know I handed it over to Cy the same day I got it, because it was made out to him. He was bridging funds or something for the vendor."

So Cyril was delaying deposits and reaping the interest, as well as taking kickbacks. It made sense.

"One more thing, Johnny. How much would you guess Cyril Lisk took home last year in commissions?"

"I don't need to guess. I know exactly. The company's small—we all know what one another earns." Johnny named a generous amount that wouldn't come anywhere close to covering Cyril's expenses.

"Thanks." Ben was satisfied. He'd listened to plenty of liars in his time, and Johnny Calvados wasn't one of them.

He got to his feet. "You've been a big help. Sorry to bother you."

"Annabelle knows about the fraud charges, right?" Johnny questioned anxiously. "I figure that's probably why you're here."

Ben nodded, noncommittal.

"Damn it all, anyway." Johnny smacked the door-jamb with his fist. "I knew I should have leveled with her and Cyril when they hired me. It's just not something you're proud to put on your résumé. See, Cy never liked me much. I figured if I said anything, the partnership would be toast. I'll have a talk with them, explain what really happened, and just hope they believe me."

"Why not let me handle it? I'll be seeing Annabelle later tonight, anyway." He'd thought it over, and he was going to have to involve her before he went any further with Lisk. That was going to be the hardest part of the whole thing for him, but he couldn't see any way around it.

Ben held out his hand, and Johnny shook it.

"Maybe we ought to have that talk about Jason one of these days," Johnny said as Ben was going out the door. "I'm going to need all the help I can get with the boy. I know he doesn't like me much, and I'd like to change that."

"Give him time and space," Ben said slowly, liking the other man's sincerity. "Jase has had lots of disappointments, and he's not about to trust anybody right off the bat. But keep trying. He'll come around. He's a good kid."

"I know that," Johnny answered with that same absolute certainty Ben had heard in his voice before. "After all, he's Daisy's son, isn't he?"

A weight seemed to drop from Ben's shoulders. Daisy and Jason were going to be fine with Johnny Calvados.

"Drop in next time you're out in Oyama, have a beer with me," Ben suggested. He found himself wishing he could stay and talk to Johnny instead of facing Annabelle.

It took him four trips on the bike around her apartment building before he got up enough nerve to go and knock at her door, and his heart was hammering when he heard her fumble at the lock.

He was here on business, he reminded himself. If anything personal was going to happen, she'd have to make the first move.

He was more determined than ever about that.

It was a matter of principle and pride.

Then she opened the door, and all he could think of was how much he'd missed her.

HER HEART STOPPED WHEN she swung the door wide and saw him there.

Her first impulse was to throw herself into his arms, but something in his face, a kind of remoteness, halted her just in time. His eyes were shuttered, as if he'd drawn a curtain down over the warmth that had always been there for her.

"Sorry to bother you, Annabelle," he said in a formal, rigid voice that must be a hangover from his police days. "Some things have come up that I think you should know about. They affect your business, and they need dealing with right away."

"Come in." She was amazed her voice worked. She turned and led the way into the living room, and when he sat in an armchair, she chose the seat farthest away from him. She folded her hands in her lap to hide the way she was trembling, and waited for him to begin.

"I know you resent me poking into your affairs, but Jason happened to tell me Johnny and Daisy are talking marriage, and I got worried." He paused, watching her; waiting, she knew, for the explosion that had come the last time they discussed her business.

She took refuge in silence and waited for whatever he was going to say next.

"I've conducted an investigation into your businesses, both Pinetree and Midas, because I figured for sure Johnny was defrauding you somehow." He was still watching her, wary of her reaction.

"And what did you find out?" She kept her voice rock steady, even though the bottom was dropping out of her stomach. The results of the audit had come just before she left the office that afternoon, and there had been problems with some of the deposits.

She knew Johnny was guilty, and she'd been agonizing over what to do about it. Cyril was in Vancouver at a realtors' conference, so she couldn't even talk it over with him.

"I found out that there's no question Cyril Lisk has been taking kickbacks on every single development project Pinetree has ever been involved with. Naturally the company's losing money, because the contractors pay him up front, and then have to pad the estimates to make any profit for themselves. So you're shelling out a lot more money than you should on every contract."

Annabelle felt as if a fist had slammed into her chest. She couldn't get her breath. She gaped at Ben, speechless. Cyril. Not Johnny at all, but Cyril. She opened her mouth and closed it again, unable to form words.

Ben held a hand up, palm out, like a traffic cop. "Before you tell me I'm all wrong—that good old Cyril wouldn't do a thing like that—remember that check that didn't get deposited when it should have? Well, my guess is that Lisk's been getting greedy. He could deposit checks like that one into a separate account and collect the interest himself. I've talked to Johnny, and I'm convinced he's telling the truth when he says he gave the check to Lisk. You told me yourself you trusted him with the banking. The only reason he got caught was because your bank manager went over the receivables with a fine-tooth comb."

She wanted to tell him about the audit, but her stomach was heaving. She drew in deep breaths and let them out again, feeling light-headed.

"There's no doubt at all Lisk's been taking the kickbacks, but we need some sort of concrete proof before we can confront him or lay charges. In my experience, guys like this always keep some kind of records for their own use. I'd like to search his office, see what we can come up with. Unless you want to go to the police and let them take over the rest of the investigation?"

The resulting scandal would be the final blow to a business already in trouble. She knew that beyond a doubt.

"I don't want the police involved—not unless it's unavoidable." Annabelle got to her feet, hoping her knees would hold her. "There's no one at the office now. I'll get my keys."

He got up, as well. "My bike's outside. I'll meet you over there in fifteen minutes."

The door closed quietly behind him, and she collapsed on the sofa, fighting the nausea that suddenly overcame her.

THERE WERE NO RECORDS in Cy's office. Feeling like the worst kind of snoop, Annabelle helped Ben go through file cabinets and desk drawers and even the wastepaper basket.

It was Ben who lifted the desk blotter and found the empty envelope. It bore the logo of an excavating company. "Morris Exc, $1,000.00" Cy had scrawled across it, along with the date. The check that had been inside was gone.

It was enough to wipe away any lingering doubts Annabelle might have entertained about Cy's innocence. She took the envelope when Ben handed it to her, and outrage began to build within her at the enormity of Cyril Lisk's betrayal.

"My guess is he forgot to take this home with him. Most likely, that's where he keeps his records—at home," Ben stated. "By itself, this isn't enough to confront him with."

The sleepless nights, the weeks of anxiety, the financial pressure she'd been under while Cyril Lisk was quietly cheating the socks off her company gave her a sense of furious purpose.

"Cyril and his wife are in Vancouver at a conference. They left yesterday and won't be back till tomorrow afternoon. He's meeting two clients here at the office at two. He probably won't show up till then. There's a spare set of keys to his house in the drawer of Hilda's desk. He always leaves them there in case of emergency."

Ben gave her a calculating look. "Are you suggesting we B and E his house?"

"It's not break and enter if we have a set of keys, is it?"

Annabelle was already at Hilda's desk. In the second drawer she found the keys, neatly tagged by efficient Hilda.

"If you decide to get out of real estate, you could have quite a career as a criminal, you know," Ben said, and for the first time since he'd appeared at her door an hour before, there was a hint of humor in his eyes, but it vanished quickly.

"We'd better take your car. The motorcycle's too conspicuous."

Together they drove to Cyril's house.

# 12

"HE'S NOT LONG ON imagination, I'll say that for Lisk. I'd have thought a safe, or at least a secret panel."

Ben flipped another page in the dark green ledger they'd found in the only locked drawer of Cyril's desk, and Annabelle traced with a forefinger the ever-increasing amount registered in the credit column.

Bitterness choked her. "No wonder Madeline wore all that ghastly jewelry and that hideous fur coat. I could never figure out why he'd have such a grasping, greedy woman as a wife. But they were the same, underneath. He just hid it better than she."

Her hand wasn't shaking the slightest bit now. She was filled with an awful rage. "This makes me furious. I can understand why people commit murder."

Ben rested a hip on the corner of the massive antique desk that took up most of the space in Cyril's dark study. "Any other alternatives come to mind? I know the bastard deserves it, but murder's not always the best revenge. And I doubt you'd get very far charging him through the courts, either."

She shot him a look, but he was idly flipping through the records of Cyril's treachery again. "This ledger may look like proof positive to us, but without statements and witnesses to back it up, it's nothing. None of the companies paying kickbacks are going to testify against him. He hasn't stolen money outright that belonged to the company. From what you've said about the audit, there's not enough evidence to even charge him. He wasn't stealing. He was just delaying the deposits."

He looked up and met her gaze with that cool, impersonal look she was beginning to hate. "It's touch and go whether he'd even be charged."

"Then what can I do? There must be something I can do.

"At the very least, I'm going to confront him with all this, the moment he appears at the office tomorrow afternoon," she said bitterly. "I want him to admit what he's done. I want him out of the partnership. I want him to know I finally understand what a vile liar and cheat he really is. Then I never, ever want to see him again." There were tears in her eyes and she swiped at them with the back of her hand. She looked around and shuddered. "Let's get out of here. This whole place reminds me of him."

She picked up the ledger and Ben led the way to the front door.

The drive back to the office was as strained as the drive to Cyril's house had been earlier. When she pulled up in the parking lot beside Ben's bike, he opened the car door to get out, then hesitated. "Annabelle, would you mind if I was there tomorrow when you tell Lisk what you know? It would be a good idea to clue Johnny in right away about what's going on. I can phone him tonight if you like. And first thing in the morning, I'd get some papers drawn up by a lawyer so Lisk can sign them right away—since he isn't the trustworthy sort. And it would be a good idea to have a couple of witnesses on hand."

"I'd appreciate having you there, Ben." She'd been trying to dredge up enough nerve to ask him. "I . . . I want to thank you for all you've done for me. I appreciate it."

"No problem. See you at noon tomorrow."

The awful, polite formality between them hurt her. She watched him get on the bike with fluid grace. He then turned and waved just before he roared off into the night. His helmet hid his face, and she couldn't see his expression.

She drove home, and for first time in weeks, she slept, locked in an exhaustion and hopelessness too deep even for dreams.

CYRIL BREEZED IN AT one forty-five the next afternoon and strolled into the office where Annabelle waited with Ben and Johnny. She stared at Cy's portly form, at the smile on his face, and she knew she could carry this off.

"Well, comrades, what's going on? Is this a private party or can anybody attend?" He smiled cheerfully at all of them.

Without preamble, Annabelle held out the ledger. "I know what's been going on, Cyril. I know about everything." She was proud of herself for the quiet, dignified way she said it.

That was as far as she got with dignity, though. All morning, she'd rehearsed what she was going to say and how, but all of a sudden she couldn't remember any of it. Her fine control snapped and her voice rose dangerously. She was vaguely aware that Ben had moved protectively close on her right, with Johnny on her left, flanking her like bodyguards. It was all she could do not to physically attack the rotund man standing in front of her.

"Damn you, Cyril Lisk. I trusted you, and you cheated me. You lied, and swindled and betrayed me and the company and Johnny, as well. How could you? How could you do this—" she shook the ledger under his nose "—and still pretend every single day that you were my friend?"

Shock and a trace of fear registered on Cyril's face as his eyes flickered from the ledger to Annabelle and then to the grim faces of the men at her side.

He was silent a moment, and then he shrugged and looked straight at Annabelle, back in full control. "Business is business, kid. It's every man for himself, like I always told you. And it seems evident you can't prove I did anything wrong, or you'd have the cops here instead of this little welcoming committee. Am I right?"

His cocky, unrepentant attitude shocked Annabelle into silence. She stared at the man she'd respected and even loved as friend, teacher and partner.

What was wrong with her, that she could have misjudged people as terribly as she had? She'd married Theodore Winslow. She'd trusted Cyril Lisk. And she'd refused Ben Baxter's love and driven him away.

Cyril's voice seemed to come from a long way off. "I suppose you expect me to walk away now, nice and quiet and humble, huh? Well, I've got news for you. If you want me out of this partnership, I'm open to negotiations, but it's going to cost you what I'm worth. Right off the top of my head, I figure my shares are worth, let's see . . ."

He named an astronomical sum, and Annabelle gasped.

"You're nothing but a thieving crook, Lisk." Johnny moved, fast and threatening, toward the other man, but Ben was faster.

He took two steps forward and casually gathered up a fistful of Cyril's Hawaiian-print shirt, lifting the portly man almost off his feet.

"Maybe we ought to renegotiate this, Lisk." Ben's voice was silky and low and lethal. "I happen to have some friends in the income-tax department who'd be very interested in how much you earn versus how much you declare. Internal revenue doesn't care how you make your dirty money, but I happen to know they care a lot that they get their fair share. And you've been spending a lot more than you said you'd been earning. Correct? There's that nice apartment building in Hawaii, and the condo in Palm Springs, and the cars and your wife's jewelry, for starters. I only had a couple of days to look into things, so I probably missed a lot." He shook Cyril like a dog shaking a rat. "Internal revenue won't miss anything, though. I've heard they get really nasty about hiding income."

Cyril was now making high, squeaking sounds in his throat, and when Ben suddenly let him go, he staggered and seemed to deflate like a balloon with the air escaping.

Ben's voice was an ominous growl. "Now, what about those terms of yours, Lisk? I think what you figure you're worth has just gone down to about zero. Am I right?"

With a hand that shook so badly he could hardly sign his name, Cyril relinquished his shares in both companies. Ben and Johnny stood over him like bloodhounds while Cyril cleared out his desk and slunk out the door. Annabelle walked over to the window and watched as his black Cadillac left the parking lot, tires screaming on the tarmac as it pulled out onto the highway and sped away.

Ben glanced at his watch. "I've got to be going. I'm glad everything ended as well as it did."

Annabelle turned toward him, longing to stop him, but afraid. If Johnny hadn't been right there, she might have tried.

"I doubt you'll have any further problems with Lisk, but I'd have the locks changed on the office as a safeguard." Ben shook Johnny's hand, but he only nodded at Annabelle—a polite impersonal nod.

"Goodbye, Annabelle. Good luck." It sounded final. He hurried out the door.

Annabelle tried to stifle the tears that were choking her. Not only had Ben saved her business, but he'd also given her back her dreams, taught her to laugh again, offered her love.

She'd pushed him away, and now he was walking out of her life.

Should she run after him, tell him how she felt about him?

"Annabelle?" Johnny put his hand on her arm in a tentative gesture. "What d'ya say you and I go out and have some lunch and talk things over? There're a lot of decisions to be made with Cyril gone, a lot of work to do to get things back in shape around here. And there're only four days left in August. Then Mr. Sam's going to be on the phone bright and early, September one, wanting to know if we were able to get Likely Cove. We need to figure out what we're going to do about that."

Strain was evident in Johnny's face. "What the hell are we going to do about it, Annabelle? Now that the bank's pulled the rug out, all I can see is that we're going to have to dump it fast, if that's even possible. Nothing's moving right now."

Johnny was shaken, just as she was, by Cyril's treachery and the ugly events of the morning. He was also worried about the business, and he had every justification to be worried.

Midas Realty and Pinetree Developments were still in serious trouble—although now, at least, they stood a fair chance of recovering. She had a responsibility—to Johnny and to the business. Her personal life would just have to wait for another few hours.

She mustered all her reserves and did her best to be businesslike and sensible for the rest of the afternoon, but the moment the workday was over, she drove to Oyama.

During the forty-minute drive, she rehearsed what she was going to say, and by the time she pulled to a stop in Ben's driveway she'd committed every last humble word to memory.

Her heart was hammering against her ribs.

As usual, Susie came rushing over to say hello, and Annabelle braced herself as the dog jumped to greet her and licked her face. Jason followed close behind, swinging the handle of the bucket he was using to feed the chickens.

"Hi-ya, Annabelle. Get down, Susie. Just shove her off. She's not supposed to jump up like that. Bad dog!" He grabbed Susie's collar and dragged her down. "Ben's not here. He flew to Edmonton an hour ago to get the alpacas. They've been released from quarantine and he's going to drive them home in a big cattle truck."

Annabelle stared at the boy, bitterly disappointed. How could Ben not be here? Why hadn't he said anything this afternoon about having to catch a plane?

The answer was crystal clear. She was no longer someone he confided in about the details of his life. She'd lost that privilege, along with so much else.

Could she ever win it back?

"I wanted to go with him," Jason was saying, "but somebody had to stay here and take care of things, and Ben says he trusts me." The boy puffed up with pride. "Hey, Annabelle, did you see the baby Clara had? C'mon over and take a look."

Battling to suppress her overwhelming disappointment, Annabelle followed Jason over to the pen. He unlocked the gate and she went inside with him.

The long-legged, long-necked baby was adorable. Annabelle knelt beside the tiny creature, running her fingers through the downy wool on her sides, stroking the long, delicate, banana-shaped ears, and marveling at the utter trust the baby and her mother displayed toward both Jason and herself. Clara stood nearby, humming to both her baby and her admirers.

"Oh, Jason, she's absolutely beautiful!"

Jason beamed. "That's what Ben says, too. He says that's why he called her Bella. He says that means beautiful in Italian." He sniggered. "But I know he really named her after you. He always calls you Bella, right? Ben told me lots of times he thinks you're real beautiful, too."

Tears came to her eyes, and Annabelle blinked them away, pretending to study little Bella so Jason wouldn't see.

"I figure she's a lot better looking than I am, Jason. She's certainly got longer eyelashes."

A few months ago, she'd have been mortally insulted if anyone had named an animal after her. Now, she was ridiculously pleased and flattered. She wanted to share her delight with Ben, and not being able to do so caused an ache inside her. The thought of driving home to an empty apartment was unbearable.

"Is your mom at home, Jason?" It had been a long while since she'd had a chance to visit with Daisy. Annabelle suddenly longed for a heart-to-heart talk with her friend.

"Yeah, she's there. She hasn't got any classes for two weeks. Then she starts the real-estate course."

"Maybe I'll drive over and say hello. You want a ride home with me?"

Jason shook his head. "I've got my bike, and I'm not finished chores yet. Besides, I always throw a ball for Susie when I'm done. She'd be disappointed if I didn't. Tell Mom I'll be home by dark, okay?"

"Okay." Annabelle smiled at the boy. He seemed to have grown taller and more gangly over the summer, and somehow he'd become her friend, too. "Ben's fortunate to have you taking care of things, Jason."

His face lit up, and he beamed at her. "See ya when Ben gets back, right?"

"When will that be, Jase?"

He shrugged. "Dunno, for sure. Driving through with the alpacas could take a while. Few days, maybe a week. Depends."

It sounded like forever.

Annabelle drove to Daisy's. Johnny's car was parked in the yard beside Daisy's Volkswagen. Annabelle's heart sank.

Selfishly, she'd been counting on Daisy being alone. She'd wanted to pour out her feelings and fears, and get back a dose of Daisy's unique advice and comfort.

It wasn't meant to be. The lovers were in the back-yard, and Annabelle felt like an intruder when she rounded the corner and saw them there.

Their chairs were side by side so they could hold hands, and Daisy had the flushed and radiant look of a woman who'd been well and thoroughly made love to very recently.

Daisy brought Annabelle ice tea, and they both welcomed her with warm affection. Johnny had filled Daisy in on the events at the office, and they discussed Cyril and his departure, but after half an hour, Annabelle invented a meeting she had to attend in Kelowna.

The warm, intimate circle the lovers unconsciously occupied made her more than ever aware of being alone.

"I've decided what to do about the development property, Johnny," she heard herself say just as she was leaving. The idea had come to her full-blown while she was sipping her tea. It scared her, but it was a solution to their financial problems—if she could pull it off.

"Tomorrow, I'm going to sell the land to Golden Circle Realty, for as much as the traffic will bear. Unless you've come up with a better idea, of course." She sounded a lot more confident than she felt.

Johnny gave her an incredulous look. "But that's Winslow's company. I thought he was the last person you'd want to sell to. I thought he was the one you wanted to beat out in the first place."

"He was." She could remember how she'd felt about Theodore—the hatred, the long-standing desire for revenge—but the intensity was gone. In the space of a summer, she realized with amazement, those feelings had faded. Now they seemed nothing more than a distant memory, without the power to hurt her anymore.

She no longer really cared much about Theodore Winslow, one way or the other. The realization surprised her.

"I guess I've changed, Johnny." She waved to them both and walked to her car, feeling as though she'd finally put aside a heavy load she'd been carrying for far too long a time.

WAITING TO MEET THEODORE the following noon at the trendy restaurant he'd suggested, Annabelle was much less confident than she'd been the night before.

After calling him early that morning and suggesting they meet for lunch, she'd pawed through her wardrobe in a panic, eventually choosing to wear a white raw-silk suit over a lemon camisole. The skirtband was loose; she must have lost weight over the summer. No wonder—her stomach seemed in a constant state of unrest.

Inexplicably, the camisole was tight across her breasts. She exchanged it for a silk knit in aquamarine.

"Hey, Annabelle, you're looking good." Theodore Winslow slid heavily into the booth across from hers. "How about a drink? It's hot enough out there to fry eggs on the sidewalk."

Kelowna was a small city. She'd seen Theodore now and then over the years at one real-estate function or another, always keeping as much distance between them as she possibly could.

"How are you, Theo?" Now that she took a good, close look at him, she saw that the portly, middle-aged man across the table bore little resemblance to the young, dynamic adventurer she'd married a dozen years before.

"Couldn't be better, couldn't be better." His eyes were puffy and his shirt collar looked too tight. He scanned the room and waved ostentatiously at a group of businessmen nearby. "City council. That's the mayor just coming in now." He waved again, and for a moment Annabelle wondered if he was going to stand up and bow.

Her anxiety about the meeting began to diminish. The man across from her could have been a stranger, for all the distance she felt from him.

The waiter appeared and Theo ordered a double Scotch.

Annabelle had ice water. She sipped at it and noticed that Theo had begun letting one side of his hair grow long so he could comb it up and over an incipient bald spot on the top. It looked peculiar, to say the least. It was a little sad, because he'd always been vain about his thick, sandy hair. He'd worn it long, tied back on his neck with a leather thong when she'd first met him.

"Well, dear, here's to old times." His voice was condescending as he raised his glass and took a healthy slug. The hair on the top didn't budge when he tossed his head back to swallow, and for a mad moment she wondered if he used crazy glue to hold the strands in place. She considered calling *him* "dear" right back, and decided it wasn't worth the effort.

They ordered their food, and Theo had a second Scotch with the low-cal salad plate.

"Gotta watch the old waistline," he said with a good-natured guffaw, forking up cottage cheese and washing it down with Scotch.

He told her his golf handicap and mentioned that he played tennis twice weekly. He managed to include the name of his club, the most expensive in town.

Annabelle nibbled at a sandwich and wondered when the powerful arch enemy she'd hated all these years had disintegrated into this rather pathetic middle-aged man.

When the time came at last to do business, she found that he was still good at dealing.

It didn't matter, because so was she. The verbal agreement they arrived at for the purchase of the development property was about what she'd hoped it might be—not nearly what Pinetree had paid, but enough to satisfy the bank until she and Johnny could recoup their losses. Theo agreed to sign papers and arrange for a transfer of funds within the week.

"Guess you got yourself in over your head on this one, huh?" He couldn't resist gloating over the deal. Annabelle couldn't have cared less.

She stood and held out her hand. "I'll call you as soon as the papers are ready."

He lumbered to his feet and held her hand a beat too long. His hand was sweaty and hot, and her skin crawled.

"Maybe we oughta get together for a drink some evening. For old times' sake, huh, Annabelle?"

She was in her car with the motor running when it dawned on her he'd been making a pass, and for the first time in days, she really laughed.

She burst through the office door, eager to tell Johnny that at least part of their problems were solved, and Hilda handed her a courier envelope.

"This just came for you. Johnny said to tell you he's sold the apartment building out in Westbank. He's over at the lawyer's now with the client, getting the papers signed." Hilda's wrinkled face creased into a smile. "Seems like things are looking up around here. It's good to see you looking so cheerful for a change, Anna-belle." The older woman had been as shocked as any of them at Cyril's duplicity.

In her office, Annabelle slipped off the jacket of her suit and hung it up, kicking off her high-heeled sandals while she mentally congratulated Johnny. The sale of the apartment building was a real boon for the busi-ness. They'd had it listed for over a year with not a sin-gle offer.

Maybe their luck had turned at last.

She visited the bathroom and then shuffled some of the papers on her desk for a while before she remem-bered the courier envelope and slit it open.

It was a deed, made out in her name. She gaped down at it, scarcely able to comprehend what it represented.

It was for a property called Likely Cove. It gave her outright ownership. It was signed by Ben Baxter.

With it was a single sheet of lined paper, the kind found in children's notebooks.

Ben had scrawled a simple message across it.

He'd written, "I love you, Annabelle. Take this and make all your dreams come true."

He'd given her what she wanted, after all—what she'd thought she needed so desperately.

She stared down at the deed, painfully aware of what an ironic, hollow victory this was.

It was Ben she wanted, not his property. Her fingers moved, grasping the corner of the deed, about to tear it up.

But as always, the decision wasn't a simple one. There was Johnny and the business to consider.

There was still time to withdraw the offer she'd made to Theo.

Mr. Sam would be phoning tomorrow morning. She and Johnny had the chance now to pursue the development, to make a tidy profit that would cancel out the company's losses once and for all, wipe away the legacy of debt Cyril had left them.

It was the very last thing in the world she wanted to do. She'd never be able to look at Likely Cove without remembering Paradise, and all it represented.

Annabelle sank back in her chair, shut her eyes and tipped her head back.

Why couldn't anything ever just be easy?

# 13

THE BETTER PART OF A week passed before Ben made it home late on a Friday evening. Getting alpacas released from quarantine, loaded into trucks, and driven across the Rockies hadn't been the easiest thing he'd ever done, and it sure as hell was challenging. The long drive had given him a chance to do some thinking about Annabelle, and as soon as he got his ten animals settled in Oyama, he was going to track her down and spell out how he felt about her, once and for all, with brutal honesty.

He'd given her Likely Cove partly because he knew she needed it if her business was going to survive. But as he drove the rumbling cattle truck across the wheat fields of central Alberta, he'd acknowledged that Likely Cove had also become a focus for all the differences between them, and he wanted to level those differences, start fresh with her. And the cove was a small price to pay for that.

As he rolled across the foothills, he concluded that pride and principles sometimes didn't matter a damn when you loved someone the way he loved Annabelle.

Deep in the Rockies, though, maneuvering his precious cargo through the glaciers of Jasper and Lake Louise, he decided that she'd have to understand and accept that he wasn't going to change his life-style. He couldn't—not even for her. He was what he was.

Descending at last into the gentle mountain ranges of the lake country near his home, he knew that he loved her—so much that it frightened him.

If they were going to have a life together, it was time to get on with it. He'd fantasized, during the endless, lonely drive, how it would be to wake up with her next to him every morning.

He'd build her a mansion on his land, if that's what she wanted, but would she mind living in Oyama and driving in to Kelowna every day to go to work?

He'd even gone so far as to fantasize a family—a couple of boys and a little girl, maybe. How he'd love a little girl.

He was trying to decide what she'd look like when he climbed the last hill toward home.

Settling ten alpacas into a strange paddock wasn't the easiest task in the world. At half-past five on Saturday morning, Susie's barking had alerted him to the fact that the alpacas, no doubt aided by devious Cupid, had somehow escaped from the compound. The animals were wandering around the orchard along with a few of the resident deer, and Ben found that rounding them up alone was a next-to-impossible task.

A desperate phone call brought Jason to the rescue, and now they had the animals penned in again, but the high-tension wire fencing Ben had strung up around the new paddocks was proving to be a problem.

"They're either gonna rub all the hair off their necks, or choke themselves to death on that wire, Ben," Jason observed. The alpacas obviously were convinced that the grass was greener outside their pen. They all had their long necks stuck through the wire, straining for mouthfuls of the same damned grass that grew inside their paddock.

"We're just going to have to replace it with chain link fencing, Jase. I'll drive into town and pick some up when the stores open this morning. But right now, let's go make some breakfast. I could use half-a-dozen cups of strong coffee and some pancakes. How about you?"

"All right. It's gonna be another hot day. I sure wish it would start to rain, then I'd feel better about starting school next week. Did you ever used to feel that way about school, Ben? Like you were trapped inside and all the sunshine was going to waste somewhere else?"

Ben knew exactly how Jason felt. He'd felt that way himself for the past while—as if all the sunshine was gone from his life.

Jason's voice took on an excited tone. "Hey, somebody's coming up the drive. I think it's Annabelle. It is her. Boy, she's sure up early, huh, Ben? I bet she's coming to see the new alpacas. I showed her Bella, the night she came out here to see you when you were gone. She really liked Bella."

Ben's heart almost thumped a hole through his rib cage. So Annabelle had driven out to see him while he was away. And she was here again, now. He ran a hand over his jaw, wishing he'd taken time to shave before he herded up the alpacas.

She pulled the little red car to a stop and got out.

She was wearing a blue cotton skirt and a plain white T-shirt with lace at the neckline, and the fresh-scrubbed, delicious morning look of her made him want to gather her into his arms right that moment and never, never let her go again.

She smiled—a tiny, tentative smile that didn't quite seem to reach her eyes. She was pale underneath the smattering of freckles across her nose.

"Morning, Ben. Hi, Jase. You guys are sure up early. Daisy phoned and told me about the alpacas." She reached back into the car and retrieved her battered briefcase, not quite meeting Ben's eyes when she straightened. "I have some documents that require your signature, Ben."

It took every ounce of discipline to hide his disappointment. She was here on business, and that was all. He'd thought there for a moment that she was going to make everything easier for him, but it seemed he was going to have to do the hard work of getting her back all by himself.

"Jase, why don't you go inside and put the coffee on? I'll be along in a minute." He wanted a chance to speak to her in private. He led the way around to the back decks and seated her on one of the chairs by the round, umbrella-shaded table. He sat down across from her and waited. He could almost feel the tension in the air.

She rummaged inside her briefcase, produced a sheet of paper, and held it out to him.

He skimmed it, and then, unable to believe his eyes, he started at the beginning and read it again.

It was a document drawn up by a lawyer in the names of Annabelle Murdoch and Ben Baxter for joint ownership of Likely Cove.

He raised his eyes and met her anxious gaze, and a wild, crazy suspicion began within him.

"I talked it over with Johnny. We decided to forget the development parcel and concentrate on local retail sales instead. I sold the parcel above the cove to Theodore Winslow's company. The deal went through yesterday."

He understood what she was telling him. She'd cut the ties with Winslow, at last. He was proud of her, and happy for her, and he wanted to tell her so, but she was still talking.

"I was wrong, Ben, about so many things. I should have trusted you and I didn't. I should have trusted my own feelings, but I was afraid." She swallowed again. "I . . . I love you, Ben."

It was a miracle. It was what he'd longed to hear her say, but it wasn't enough. His world was here, and he didn't know whether she could accept that.

"I love you too, Bella—more than I can say. But I have to know what kind of life you want." Maybe she couldn't live like this, dogs and llamas and Jason and poultry all over the place, stuck out here in the boonies.

Maybe she loved him, but didn't want to go further than that; didn't want to commit to marriage. From what she'd told him, her first marriage had left her scarred pretty deeply. Maybe the scars would never heal, and another marriage wasn't what she wanted at all.

And God, *he* wanted it. He didn't think he could settle for anything less.

"You're not making this very easy, Ben Baxter." She drew a deep breath and let it out in a long, shaky sigh.

"I want to live out here with you, if you'll have me," she confessed. "I want to ride on the back of your motorcycle, and go swimming, and...and watch you make wine. I want to let Johnny take over more of the business so I have time. I think maybe Daisy will come to work for us when she gets her license."

She met his eyes with an earnestness that moved him. "I've got a bit of money saved, Ben. We wouldn't be rich, but we'd manage."

He swallowed the lump that rose in his throat. He would set her straight about his finances, but for now, her offer to support him touched him to the roots of his being.

She put her hand on the agreement still between them on the table. "I was going to add a conditional clause about a honeymoon on Paradise Island, but lost my nerve."

Happiness bubbled inside him like the finest summer wine. He could hardly contain his joy. He had an insane urge to shout at the top of his lungs, to stand up with his arms spread wide and roar out over the entire valley that Bella loved him.

"You'll marry me, then, Bella?" The words came out more in a whisper than a roar.

She nodded. "I certainly will." He started to get up, unable to wait another instant before he took her in his arms, but she put a hand on his arm and stopped him.

"There's just one other thing." This time the smile on her lips was reflected in her dark brown eyes, and he knew whatever she had to say was nothing serious—nothing that would come between them.

"What's that, Bella?"

"I went to see the doctor yesterday, Ben. I think we ought to get married right away, because he says I'm pregnant."

This time, there was no containing his elation. He threw his head back and let the wordless sound of his rapture burst into the morning air, filling the valley and echoing back, alarming the alpacas and setting Susie to barking.

Jason came running out to see what was the matter, but he made a gagging noise in his throat and quickly retreated inside, because Annabelle and Ben were kissing.

They didn't even notice him. Well, he might as well go ahead and eat cereal. The way things were going, who knew how long it would be before Ben remembered the pancakes?

# This month's
# irresistible novels from

## *Temptation*

**THE OTHER WOMAN  by Candace Schuler**

This is the first in a blockbusting **Hollywood Dynasty** trilogy.

The newspapers were full of gossip about Tara Channing—TV's sexiest seductress and star of the new movie *The Promise*—and her surprising relationship with Gage Kingston whose family was a legend in Hollywood. He had sworn never to fall for another actress, and Tara had had her own share of heartache, too. Would their love survive all the media attention?

**YOU GO TO MY HEAD by Bobby Hutchinson**

With her company on the verge of bankruptcy, the only person who could save Annabelle Murdoch's dream was Ben Baxter. But, sexy, laid-back Ben wasn't interested in business. He was interested only in awakening her to the pleasure of life and love…

**LOVESTORM  by JoAnn Ross**

Saxon Carstairs was a loner, but his isolation was shattered when gorgeous Madeline washed up half-dead on his beach. Helpless and unable to remember anything beyond her name, Madeline aroused all Sax's instincts—protective, heroic *and* carnal.

**THE MISSING HEIR by Leandra Logan**

Responsible for locating Douglas Ramsey's missing heir, Caron Carlisle was shocked when the person who said he could solve the mystery turned out to be Rick Wyatt—the man who had broken Caron's heart years before.

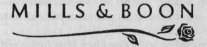

# A Tempting FREE Offer
# from Mills & Boon

We'd love you to become a regular reader of Temptations and discover
the modern sensuous love stories that have made this such a very
popular series. To welcome you we'd like you to have 4 TEMPTATION
books, a CUDDLY TEDDY and a MYSTERY GIFT absolutely FREE.

Then, every month you could look forward to receiving 4 brand new
Temptations delivered to your door for just £1.95 each, postage and
packing FREE. Plus our FREE Newsletter filled with of author news,
competitions, special offers and much more.

It's easy. Send no money now.
Simply fill in the coupon below and send it to-
**Reader Service, FREEPOST, PO Box 236,
Croydon, Surrey CR9 9EL.**

No Stamp Required

# Free Books Coupon

**Yes!** Please rush me 4 FREE Temptations and 2 FREE gifts! Please also
reserve me a Reader Service subscription. If I decide to subscribe I can
look forward to receiving 4 Temptations for just £7.80 each month,
postage and packing FREE. If I decide not to subscribe I shall write to you
within 10 days. I can keep the free books and gifts whatever I choose.
I may cancel or suspend my subscription at any time. I am over 18
years of age.

Ms/Mrs/Miss/Mr _____ EP73 T

Address _____

_____

Postcode _____ Signature _____